THE SHEIKH'S PREGNANT PRISONER

BY
TARA PAMMI

MILLS & BOON

Published in Great Britain 2016
By Mills & Boon, an imprint of HarperCollins*Publishers*
1 London Bridge Street, London, SE1 9GF

© 2016 Tara Pammi

ISBN: 978-0-263-91589-1

Our policy is to use papers that are natural, renewable and recyclable products and made from wood grown in sustainable forests. The logging and manufacturing processes conform to the legal environmental regulations of the country of origin.

Printed and bound in Spain
by CPI, Barcelona

THE SHEIKH'S PREGNANT PRISONER

For my lovely and wonderful editor, Pippa—
for these ten books and many, many more to come.

CHAPTER ONE

COULD HE BE DEAD? Could someone as larger than life as Zafir be truly gone? Could someone she had known for two months, someone she had laughed with, someone she had shared the deepest intimacies with, be gone in the blink of an eye?

Lauren Hamby pressed her hand to her stomach as dread weighed it down.

It had been the same for the past two days. The more she saw of the colorful capital city of Behraat and the destruction the recent riots had wreaked, the more she saw Zafir everywhere.

But now, staring at the centuries-old trade center building, every nerve in her vibrated. The answer she had been seeking for six weeks was here, she could feel it in her bones. All she had was his name and description but she was desperate to find out what had happened to him.

Desperate to find out about the man who had somehow come to mean more than just a lover. More than a friend, even.

The richly kept grounds were a lush contrast to the stark silence in the city. The glittering rectangular shallow pool of water lined on either side by mosaic tiles and flanked by palm trees showed her strained reflection. She walked the concrete-tiled path laid out between the pool's edge and the perfectly cut lush lawn, her heart hammering against her rib cage.

Marble steps led to the enormous foyer with glinting

mosaic floors, soaring, circular ceiling and, she couldn't help smiling, palm trees in giant pots.

There was so much to look at, so much to breathe in that the sights and sounds around her dulled the edge during the day. But at night, the grief pushed in with vehemence, pressing images of *him* growing up in this country.

She saw him in every tall, stunning man, remembered the pride and love with which he'd painted a picture of Behraat to her.

"You coming, Lauren?"

Her friend David had spent the past few days capturing footage about the recent riots in the city.

She looked up and averted her face as he pointed his camcorder at her. "Stop filming me, David. Is my asking to see the records of people who died in the riots so necessary to your documentary on Behraat?"

Her gaze moved past the reception area, taking in the spectacular fountain in the middle of the hall, the water shimmering golden against the light shed by the orange, filigreed dome.

A hum of activity went on behind the gleaming marble reception area.

Her rubber soles made no sound as she walked past the fountain toward the reception desk. The glass elevator pinged down, a group of men exiting.

A quiet hush descended over the activity. Her nape prickling, Lauren turned, the sudden shift in the very air around her raising goose bumps on her skin. Six men stood in a circle in front of the elevator, all dressed in the traditional long robes. One man, the tallest among the group, addressed the rest in Arabic.

His words washed over Lauren, the tenor of his tone harsh and unyielding. It whispered over her skin like a familiar caress.

Rubbing her palms over her midriff, she tried to quell

the sudden shiver. She turned back toward David, who was filming the group of men with arrested attention. The tall man turned, bringing himself directly into her line of vision.

Lauren stilled, her heartbeat deafening to her ears.

Zafir.

The red-and-white headdress covered his hair, rendering his features starker than usual. His words resonated with authority, power, his mouth set into a hard line.

He was not dead.

Relief was like a storm, rippling and cascading over her. She wanted to throw her arms around him, touch the sharp angles of his face. She wanted to…

A cold chill seeped into her very bones even though she was wearing a long-sleeved T-shirt and loose trousers to respect the cultural norms of Behraat.

Zafir was unharmed.

In fact, he'd never looked more in his element. Yet she hadn't heard a word from him in six weeks.

She moved toward the group, an incessant pounding in her head driving away every sane thought. Adrenaline laced with fury pumped through her. The man standing closest to her turned around, alerting her presence to the group. One by one, they all turned.

Her breath suspended in her throat, her hands shook. The few seconds stretched interminably. A hysteric bubble launched into her throat.

Zafir's gold-flecked gaze met hers, the sheer force of his personality slamming into her.

Everything else around her dulled as the explosive chemistry that had punctuated every moment of their affair sparked into life, a live wire yanking her closer.

There wasn't a trace of pleasure in his gaze.

No shock in it.

But there was no guilt either.

The fact that he felt no remorse whatsoever fueled her fury. She'd shed tears over him, she'd reduced herself to a shadow of worry over him and he didn't even feel guilt.

The men stared with interest as he stepped toward her. Two guards flanked him at a little distance.

Why did Zafir have guards?

The question shot through her and fell into nothingness like dust. His dark sensuality swathed her. Her skin shivered with awareness, her stomach churned with every step that they took toward each other.

The intoxicating power of his masculinity, her intimate knowledge of that leanly honed body, everything coiled around her, binding her immobile under his scrutiny. He stopped at arm's reach, his mouth a hard slash in that stunning face, the burnished, coppery skin a tight mask over his features.

A regal movement of his head, his nod was barely an acknowledgment and so much a dismissal. "Ms. Hamby, what brings you to Behraat?"

Chilling cold filled her veins.

Ms. Hamby? He was calling her Ms. Hamby? After everything they had shared, he spoke to her as if she was a stranger?

Every little hurt Lauren had patched over since she'd been a little girl ripped open at that indifference. "After the way you left, that's what you have to say to me?"

A taut nerve throbbed in his temple but that golden gaze remained infuriatingly sedate. He looked so impossibly remote, as harsh and bleak as the desert she'd heard so much about. "If you have a complaint to register with me," he said, as now a thread of temper flashed into his perfectly polite tone, "you need an appointment, Ms. Hamby. Like the rest of the world."

His dismissal scraped her raw with its politeness but she

held on to her temper. *Somehow.* "An appointment? You're kidding me, right?"

"No. I do not...*kid.*" A step closer and she could see something beneath that calm. Shock? Displeasure? Indifference? "Do not make a spectacle of yourself, Lauren."

A shard of pain ricocheted inside her, stealing her breath.

"Don't make a scene, Lauren."

"Grow up and understand that your parents have important careers, Lauren."

"Swallow your tears, Lauren."

Her heart beating a wild tattoo inside her chest, memories and voices swirling through her head like some miniature ghosts, Lauren covered the last step between her and Zafir and slapped him.

His jaw jerked back, the crack of the slap shattering the silence like a clap of thunder.

The sound of quick footsteps pierced the haze of her fury, her hand jarring painfully at the impact, her breathing rough. Angry commands spoken in Arabic rang around them.

But she...it was as if she was functioning in a world of her own.

Something ferocious gleamed in his eyes then.

Oh, God, what had she done?

Caught in that flare, Lauren shivered, something hot twisting low in her belly. His long fingers dug into her forearms as he jerked her toward him, the scent of sandalwood and musk drenching her. "Of all the—"

An urgent whisper spoken in rapid Arabic rattled behind them. Zafir's fingers instantly relented. His gaze raked her, before the fire of his emotions slowly seeped out, settling that indifferent mask into that lethal face.

When those golden eyes met hers again, it was like looking at a stranger—a forbidding, dangerous, contemptuous stranger.

"Your Highness…let security deal with the woman."

Your Highness? Security?

The adrenaline ebbed away, leaving her cold.

Zafir barked out a command, something short and hard in Arabic and then stepped back.

Cold sweat trickled down her back as she looked around. The most unholy silence enveloped her, and everyone watched her with curiosity and contempt.

Two men with discreet-looking guns flanked her. "Zafir, wait," she called out, but he'd already turned his back on her.

Her gaze followed the elevator's ascent, but he didn't look at her, not once. She tried to step back, only to find her every move blocked.

What nightmare had she walked into? Where was David?

Trying to stem the panic bubbling inside her, she turned and noticed an older man who spoke to the guard. "What the hell is going on?"

The man's eyes chilled. "You're under arrest for attacking the Sheikh of Behraat."

Zafir Al Masood stalked out of the meeting with the High Council. His displeasure must have been evident in his face because even the most audacious members quickly shuffled out of his way.

For the first time in six weeks, the outrageous complaints from the council pricked him.

Who was the woman? How could a woman, a Western woman, an American at that, have such familiarity with him as to strike him? Was he going to bring the Western world's wrath on Behraat?

Was he going to doom Behraat for a woman like his father had done?

He entered the elevator, hit the button to hold it there.

Fury and frustration pumped in his veins as he sought to control his temper.

The glass walls around him reflected his image back at him, forcing him to take stock. Forcing him to swallow his bitterness, as he had done for the past six years.

Did they see a glimpse of his father, the great Rashid Al Masood, the man who had brought Behraat out of the dark ages, in him?

Would he be never allowed to forget that his father had only acknowledged him as his son when he had needed a different crown prince, thanks to his corrupted half brother Tariq?

Once upon a time, he would have been glad to hear that his father's blood flowed in his veins. But now...now that he was spending his life paying for his mistake...

He cursed the wretched High Council and its power to elect the High Sheikh. Maybe if the bunch of corrupt cowards had spoken up during Tariq's regime, Behraat wouldn't be in this state now.

But with Rashid's strict regulations blown apart, they had been busy stuffing their pockets with Tariq's bribes while he had ruined relations with neighboring countries, destroyed peace treaties and violated trade agreements...

Yet they used any reason to doubt *his* rule over Behraat, harped on and on about the separation of tribes from the state.

As if it was his mistake and not his father's.

Zafir headed straight to the situation room, determined to stomp them out. Much as he hated his father for bringing him up as a favored orphan, he couldn't turn a blind eye to Behraat. Even before he had learned about his birth, duty had been filled in his very blood.

This was his father's legacy to him.

Not love, not pride, not even the knowledge of his mother, but this infernal sense of duty toward Behraat.

Lauren's face on the huge plasma screen monitor brought him to a sudden halt.

Something twisted deep and hard in his gut…a hard thrum in his very muscle, an echo of a primal need that he couldn't fathom to this day…

That plump bottom lip caught between her teeth, her complexion paler than usual. Blue shadows marred the beauty of wide-set black eyes. The scarf she had used earlier to cover her hair loosely was gone, her black hair cut to fall over her forehead, once again hiding her entire face from him.

The long-sleeved cotton T-shirt molded the curve of her breasts. She sat with her fingers entwined on top of the table, her posture straight, reckless defiance in every line.

Defiant and honest, sensuous and wary, from the moment he had set eyes on her, Lauren had ensnared him.

At his command, his special security force had locked her up, confiscated everything from her. Punishment meted out to anyone who was suspected of being a threat to his new rule. And all the evidence they had gathered since didn't bode well for her either.

But he couldn't shake off the betrayal, the hurt that had glittered when she had looked at him. He had wanted to kiss her. He'd wanted to plunder her mouth until the betrayal etched into her face turned into arousal.

"She planned the charade," Arif said in his matter-of-fact tone. "She clearly means to exploit your weakness in indulging in an affair with her. You should have mentioned her to me after you returned so that I—"

"No."

Still transfixed by the sight of her, Zafir scrubbed a hand over his face.

There was no place for regret. There was no place for softness, in his feelings or in his actions. There was no choice to be anyone but himself.

Already he'd made a mistake, somehow he'd let her get too close.

"What would be her motivation, Arif?" he asked the older man. His father's oldest friend, Arif was now his biggest ally.

"She walks around the trade center with a journalist friend who knew you would be present, Zafir. It's all planned," Arif spat out, with a vehemence that had been nurtured over a lifetime for women, foreign or otherwise.

Zafir remained quiet, giving the doubts that polluted his thoughts free rein.

The few members of staff present at the trade center had already been pledged into silence. He had offered an explanation to the High Council—to keep the peace for Behraat's sake.

Her bow-shaped mouth was pinched, her shoulders strained under the weight of her feigned defiance. "Did they find him?"

The older man's disquiet was answer enough.

Zafir switched off the monitor, taking away the temptation messing with his head.

"We need to contain this as soon as possible. If that video falls into the hands of the media…" Arif continued, letting his silence speak for the consequences.

"We might have a full-scale riot on our hands again," Zafir finished. Tariq had used too many women, bloated with power and Zafir couldn't be seen in the same light.

If they didn't find the video and contain it, what little trust he had gained of the people of Behraat could be blown to smithereens.

Already, the High Council was questioning his proposals for change, looking for ways to skew public perception of him. "I'll talk to her. No one else," he said, wondering if he had misjudged the first woman to mess with his head in…ever.

* * *

How dare he lock her up?

Lauren eyed the camera in the top corner of the room. She wanted to march toward it, stick her face in it and demand they release her. But it would only waste her dwindling energy.

The sheer fury she had been running on was crashing already. Misery gnawed at her.

She turned her attention to the small room with its austere white walls and concrete floor. The sterile smell of the room made her empty stomach heave. A window boarded shut with cheap plastic and a faded plastic chair and table graced the room. The other end of the spectrum from the magnificent foyer and reception hall where she'd stood in awe only a couple of hours ago.

Even if she wanted to delude herself that it was all some ghastly mistake, the gritty reality of the room stopped her.

She held her shoulders rigid. But each passing minute filled her with increasing dread and confusion. The old man's words rang in her ears.

Zafir, the Sheikh of Behraat?

It sounded straight out of a nightmare, yet how else could she explain all this?

She rubbed her eyes and swallowed, her throat dry and scratchy like sandpaper. They had taken her backpack, her cell phone. She thought longingly of the bottle of water in there and even the granola bar she usually hated.

The knob turned as the door was fiddled with on the outside.

Her muscles tensed up, her lungs expanding on a huge breath.

Zafir stepped into the room. She sagged against the chair, saw the tight line of his mouth and instantly pulled herself back up.

He had ordered his minions to lock her up. Just because he was here didn't mean *anything*, she told herself sternly.

He cast a look at the camera at the top wall. The tiny orange flicker went out.

Apparently, all it took was a blink of an eye from him and the world rearranged itself.

He closed the door behind him, and leaned against it.

His gaze swept over her, noting everything about her with a chilling thoroughness.

The traditional attire was gone yet he felt no more familiar than the cold stranger she had slapped so foolishly. A white cotton shirt folded back at the cuffs revealed strong forearms, the burnished bronze of his skin a startlingly stunning contrast against it.

Black jeans outlined the hard strength of those muscular legs, legs that had pinned and anchored her in the most intimate of acts, a mere couple of hours before he had stepped out of her life.

The Zafir she had known in New York had still been a mystery, but he'd been a kind, caring man. Not friendly but she'd felt safe with him, even after knowing him for only an hour.

Not straightway approachable after the way she'd ripped into him at the ER, but he'd still been a gentleman.

Not exactly the boy-next-door type and yet he'd laughed with her.

Had all that been just a mask to get her into bed?

He prowled into the room and leaned against the opposite wall, forcing her to raise her gaze. Her stomach was tied up in knots, but she refused to let him intimidate her.

Standing up, she moved behind the chair and mirrored his stance.

He folded his hands and pinned her with that hard gaze. "Why are you here, Lauren?"

"Ask your thugs that question." She gripped the back of

the chair with shaking hands, and tilted her chin up. "*Sorry, I mean, your guards.*"

He raised a brow, quiet arrogance dripping from every pore. *How had she not seen this cloak of power he wore so effortlessly?* "This is not the time to play with the truth."

"Look who's talking about truth," she said, anger replacing the dread. "Is it true? What that man said?"

An eternity passed while his gaze trapped hers. But she saw the truth in it.

In fact, the truth or a shadow of it had been present all along.

In his tortured words whenever he spoke of Behraat, in the anguish in his eyes when they had watched a TV segment about the old sheikh still in coma, in the pride that resonated in his voice when he spoke of how Behraat had emerged as a developing country under the sheikh's regime.

Even in that sense of stasis she had sensed in him, as though he was biding his time.

His very presence was a ticking powerhouse in the small room. He shrugged. Such a casual gesture for something that shook her world upside down. "Yes."

The single word grew in the space between them, bearing down upon her the consequences of her own actions.

Her throat dried up, every muscle in her quivered. All the stories she had heard from a fascinated David about Behraat, of the ruling family, they coalesced in her mind, shaking loose everything she had believed of Zafir.

She stared at him anew. "If you're the new sheikh, that means you're…"

"The man who ordered the arrest of his brother so that he can rule Behraat. The man who celebrated victory on the eve of his brother's death." His words echoed with a razor-sharp edge. "But be very careful. You've already committed one mistake. I might not be so lenient again."

CHAPTER TWO

"LENIENT?" LAUREN GLARED at him, hating the tremor she couldn't contain at the casual power in his words. "You had your thugs throw me here without hearing a word I had to say."

"If you were anyone else...the punishment would have been much worse."

"I slapped you. It's not a capital crime."

"You slapped me in front of the High Council who thinks women should stay at home, that women need to be protected from the world, and from their own weaknesses."

There was no smoothness to his words now. They reverberated with cutting hostility. "That's archaic."

"Fortunately for you, I agree. Women are just as capable of deception, of manipulation as any man I've known."

Lauren stared at him. "So you're a misogynist as well as being a sheikh? I don't know how much more of this I can handle."

Something entered his gaze. "This is not New York, Lauren. Nor am I an average Joe."

"No, you're not," she whispered. Even in New York, she hadn't made the mistake of thinking he was an average man.

A small-scale exporter, he'd told her, struggling to keep his place in Behraat because of the changing political clime. The gleam of interest in his eyes—six feet of stunning, sexy, jaw-droppingly arrogant man's interest in her, averagely attractive ER nurse, who'd long ago chosen a life of non-adventure and boring normalcy, because it was safe—it had gone straight to her head.

She'd swallowed his lies all too willingly.

Instead, he *was* the ruler of a nation and, if the media was to be believed, one who had seized power from the previous sheikh. He was the very embodiment of power and ambition she despised, far from the rootless man she had thought him to be.

The black-and-white tiles swam in front of her eyes. She slid into the chair in a boneless heap, tucked her head down between her knees and forced herself to breathe.

The fine hairs on her neck prickled, the air coated with an exotic scent that her traitorous body craved all too easily. Standing over her, his presence was a dark shadow stealing every bit of warmth from her.

His long fingers landed on her nape and her skin zinged. "Lauren?"

The concern edging into those words tugged at her, but she resisted its dangerous quality. Because it was reluctant at best. "Don't pretend you care."

Shock flared in his gaze. At least, that's what her foolish mind told her. But when she looked back at him, it was gone. Before she could move, he trapped her behind the table, his arms on either side of her head. "Did you know already?"

"Know what?" Her answer croaked out of her, every cell in her pulsing with awareness at his proximity.

Her gaze fell on the thin scar that stretched from the corner of his mouth to his ear, on the left side. The memory of tracing the scar with her tongue, the taste of his skin, the powerful shudder that had gone through him, it all came back to her in a heated rush.

"Look at me when I'm speaking to you," he said, his tone dark and gravelly.

More than impatience colored his tone. She pulled her

gaze upward, her stomach doing a funny flip. His nostrils flared. The same memory danced in his eyes, making the irises a darkly burnished gold.

With a curse that reverberated around them, he clamped his jaw, until the memory and the gold fire was purged from those eyes.

The ruthlessness of his will was a slap.

She was tired, hungry, and her composure was hanging by a very fine thread. All she wanted to do was crawl into her bed and never look at the world again.

"What did I know, Zafir?"

"Did you know who I was? Is that why you slapped me and had your friend record the whole thing?"

Her sluggish brain took several seconds to react. When it did, it destroyed the barrage of unwanted memories and their effect on her. "What the hell does that mean?"

He bent down toward her, swallowing her personal space. Until their noses were almost touching and his breath fanned over her heated skin. "Your journalist friend David had a tiny camcorder and shot the whole...*incident*."

"So? Which part of the word *journalist* confuses you?" she said, confusion swirling within her. "He was running that thing all day..."

"Did he know what you were about to do? Did you plan it?"

His voice was no more than a raspy whisper yet each word dripped with menace.

Shredded everything she'd ever felt for him. "Is that how much you know me?"

Zafir ruthlessly tuned out the hurt resonating in Lauren's words.

The feel of her soft, warm flesh under his fingers was already disturbing his equilibrium.

His muscles tightened, his blood became sluggish and

the spiraling desire to kiss her mouth was a relentless hum in his veins.

He closed his eyes, and let the pictures of Behraat from six weeks ago swim in front of his eyes…the people who had died in the riots, the destruction Tariq had wrought on it. The mindless carnage instantly took the edge off his physical hunger.

A sense of balance returned to him, a cruel but efficient tether to control his body. He swept his gaze over her, letting the harsh reality of his life creep into his words. "Do we really know each other, Lauren? Except for what we like in—"

Pink seeped into her cheeks, her fiery gaze shooting daggers at him. "Stop it, Zafir."

"We knew each other for two months. I brought Huma to the ER. She told you I was…rich and you pursued me for a donation. You recklessly challenged me and I…rose to it. Against my better instincts, I started an affair. The fact that I hadn't been with a woman in a few months could have been one factor."

He continued like the ruthless bastard he was, refusing to let her pale face, the way she retreated from him, the way she shrank into the wall as though she couldn't bear to be touched by even his shadow, thwart him. "And we continued to sleep with each other because it suited us both."

He tucked away a distracting lock of hair from her cheek and she flinched. "So no, I don't know what you're capable of.

"What I do know is that you were always, what is the word, *chummy* with the press. That reporter friend David, that lawyer, Alicia and you…"

She ran long, trembling fingers over her forehead. "To set up an abuse shelter in Queens. I have nothing to gain by exposing your true colors to the world."

Frustration made his words harder. "I need that video, Lauren. The current political climate of Behraat is volatile. Even something as simple as a lover's tiff can be interpreted in so many different ways. My...predecessor abused his power, toyed with women as if they were his personal playthings. Your *act* questions my credibility, paints me in the same mold as him."

She shot her hand out, her slender fingers spread out, defiance shining out of her gleaming gaze as she ticked off her fingers. "Abuse of power? *Check*. Toys with women as though they were personal playthings? *Check*. It seems you're the perfect man for the job, Zafir."

His skin crawled to think she would cast him in the same mold as Tariq. "I've never treated you with anything other than respect."

"*Respect*?" The words boomeranged in the sterile room, mocking him. "If you respected me, you wouldn't be treating me like a criminal, questioning my actions, you wouldn't have walked out in the middle of the night and disappeared.

"The only thing missing was a bunch of cash on the nightstand and a recommendation to your friends."

"*Enough*. How dare you speak as if you sold yourself to me?"

"Because that's what *you're* implying, Zafir," Lauren shouted back at him. With an increasing sense of emptiness, she fell against the wall.

He trapped her against it, his hot gaze burning, his body a seething cauldron of aggression and sensual intent. There was no control now, only a sense of possession. She had truly angered him and still, Lauren didn't feel fear. Not when he stood close like that.

Silly, stupid Lauren.

"Is that why you did it? Because you're angry with me, you thought to teach me a lesson?"

"You know nothing about me. And I'm realizing how little I know you."

"You have no idea what you have done, Lauren. Are you ready to face the consequences? To take responsibility when another riot begins?"

She'd already learned enough about the atrocities suffered by the people of Behraat. And the sooner this nightmare was over, the sooner she would be able to leave.

She clutched on to the thought like a mantra. "Even though it isn't something I should have to explain, I will. Your claim that David and I planned…this whole thing is ridiculous. He doesn't even know about our affair."

"Then why did he run, Lauren? Why not wait to find out what happened to you?"

"Maybe because against your claims to the contrary, you seem to be walking exactly the same path as the old sheikh. You had your men seize me for a mere slap, Zafir. Can you blame him? What would he do with that video anyway? Put it on YouTube?"

His gaze hardened and she realized it was exactly the thing he wanted to avoid. He pulled her cell phone out of his pocket and slid it into her hand. "Call him. Ask him to meet you in the front lobby and bring his camcorder."

"Why?"

He glared at her. "So that we can delete that video."

"I told you. Even if David recorded it, it would be by accident. He would never do anything to hurt me. I know him."

A vein stretched taut at his temple, something hot and indecent uncoiling in his eyes. "Is that as well as you knew me or even better?"

There were so many things wrong with that question that she couldn't sift through the nuances for a minute. "What…does that mean?"

"You fell into my bed three days after we met. You traveled halfway round the world to see a man who walked out on you. I will not put much stock in your judgment right now."

A soft whimper fell from her mouth and Lauren hated herself just as much as she hated him.

Her judgment? He was using their weakness, their utter lack of control when it came to each other against her?

"You're manipulative too, great." She whispered the words softly, slowly, as though she needed to believe them herself.

A headache was beginning to blur her vision. "David isn't even aware of our…liaison," she said, intent on making him understand. "When he told me he was traveling to Behraat, I persuaded him to let me join him, made him wait until my visa was through. He didn't even know why I was coming."

"Why?"

"Why what, Zafir?"

"Why *did* you come to Behraat?"

Because I'm a silly, sentimental fool. Because, even after all these years, I still didn't learn.

He was right. Her usual common sense had taken a hike from the minute she had woken that morning six weeks ago and found him gone. But she'd acted the fool enough.

"I thought you were dead, Zafir." The hollow ache she had battled for six weeks resonated around them. "I came to see the Behraat that you told me so much about. I came to Behraat to mourn you."

He flinched and took a step back. Shock radiated from him.

"I saw the news coverage of the riots. When I didn't hear anything from you, when they reported the number of civilian casualties, I thought you had died fighting for your country and its people," she paused to breathe, to pull air past the lump that seemed to have wedged in her throat like a rock. She rubbed her fingers over her eyes, feeling incredibly tired. "But I'm such a fool, aren't I? If you had cared, you could have picked up the phone, *no wait*, you could have barked a command like you did before, and one of your thugs could have informed me that you were alive. That you were through with me."

He didn't blink, didn't move, just stared at her. Had he thought it meant nothing to her? *Had she meant nothing to him?*

"I never promised you anything, Lauren."

She nodded and the movement cost her everything she had. "As you pointed out so clearly a few minutes ago, it was an affair at best, an exchange of sex." She laughed through the tears edging into her eyes, through the haze of something clouding her eyes. All of a sudden, she felt woozy, as if there wasn't enough oxygen in the room to breathe. "I've realized that the man I came to mourn doesn't exist.

"Or if he did, he's truly dead."

Her words hit Zafir like a fist to his gut, rendering everything inside him still. The man he'd been with her, he had been neither the orphan nor the ruler.

He'd been just Zafir, free to pursue whatever he wanted.

But not anymore. Never again.

She licked her lips and swallowed visibly, her skin losing the little color she had. "Now, unless your plan is to torture me, in which case I demand a lawyer, please order one of your thugs to bring me some water. My throat feels like it's on fire."

Her gaze unfocused, she swayed on her feet and slid down the wall in a tangle of limbs.

Zafir caught her before she hit the floor, his heart pounding.

Propping her up, he tugged her close, pushed the silky

strands of her hair away from her forehead. She was burning up and dehydrated.

It could happen to anyone visiting such a hot clime for the first time, but her fainting was a direct result of his actions. Because she had been locked up the whole morning without water. On his command.

With her body slumped against his, he pulled his phone out and called Arif.

He traced the stubborn angle of her jaw with his finger, mesmerized by the contrast of his rough, brown hand over her delicate soft skin. That was it.

She had *mesmerized* him the moment he had set eyes upon her. Stunning features, alabaster skin and a sensuous mouth that could make a man forget he wasn't allowed something as frivolous as a blazing hot affair.

And even if he had somehow resisted her beauty, her biting tongue and no-nonsense attitude had won him over.

He had never met a woman like her before.

But she'd been a distraction, a respite, all that he could ever have. So he had walked away when it was time for him to return to Behraat.

But, why hadn't he, as she'd so recklessly demanded, told her he was through with her? A simple phone call would have done it…why hadn't he been able to let go?

As the door opened behind him, he lifted her in his arms and laid her on the stretcher brought in by his personal medical staff. He shook his head as Arif opened his mouth. They waited in silence as the two paramedics checked her vitals.

He couldn't let her go, not until he found the video footage. But he refused to lock her up.

"Put her in the extra suite in my wing. Plant someone from my personal guard outside her suite and ask Dr. Farrah to give her a thorough checkup."

All three men froze around him. His command went

against one of the traditional customs of Behraat. No un-married woman strayed near the edges, even by mistake, of a man's quarters.

Arif said, "We can send her to the women's clinic in the city and still have a guard there."

"No."

Letting Lauren wake up in some unknown clinic amid strangers when this was all his fault, that was inexcusable, even for him.

He wanted her close, somewhere she could be watched without causing a fuss and curiosity, which she undoubt-edly would anywhere else.

And he was no normal man like he had told her. He was not the favored orphan anymore either. He was the sheikh, and he was damned well going to use, or abuse—he didn't care which—his power in this.

"Do as I command, Arif."

Stealing one last look at her, he turned and headed to-ward the elevator, Lauren's words echoing in his ears.

"The man I mourned doesn't exist. Or if he did, he's truly dead."

How close she'd come to the truth. That carefree, reck-less, indulgent man he'd been in New York, he truly didn't exist.

CHAPTER THREE

LAUREN OPENED HER eyes slowly, feeling a sharp tug at her wrist. Her mouth felt woolly as if she had fallen asleep with cotton stuffed into it. It took her a moment to focus around the strange room. Feeling a little frayed, she propped herself on her elbows and scooted into a sitting position.

She was lying on a huge bed on the softest scented cotton sheets. The subtle scent of roses tickled her nostrils. A dark red tapestry hung on the opposite wall while sheer silk curtains fluttered at the breeze. Her whole apartment in Queens could fit into the suite, she thought, awed by the magnificence of the surroundings.

"It is nice to see some color in your cheeks," said a voice near the foot of the bed in heavily accented English.

The IV tube tugged at her wrist as Lauren moved.

A woman laid a cool hand against Lauren's forehead and nodded. She wore a bright red tunic with a collar and long sleeves, and black trousers underneath it. Her hair was tied into a ponytail at the back. Her skin, a shade lighter than Zafir's rich copper tone, shone with a vibrancy that made Lauren feel like a pale ghost.

"The fever is gone. Would you like something to drink?"

When Lauren nodded, instead of handing the glass to her, the woman tucked one hand at Lauren's neck and held it to her mouth with the other. The cool liquid slid against her throat, bringing back feeling into her mouth. Feeling infinitely better, Lauren looked at her. "Where am I?"

A little line appeared in the woman's smooth forehead. "The royal palace."

Holding her growing anxiety at bay, Lauren studied the suite again. Rich, vibrant furnishings with hints of gold greeted her eyes. A high archway lighted with bronze torches led into the balcony on her right, from which she could see the turrets and domes of the palace.

First, he had her locked up accusing her of conspiracy, and now he had staff waiting on her?

She ran a finger over her dry, cracked lips. Her blouse was creased and her cream trousers looked dirty. "I've never fainted in my life before. If you remove the IV, I'd like to wash up. And then leave."

The woman shook her head. "That's not possible."

After the day she'd had, Lauren was in no mood to be ordered around. "Excuse me, but who are you?"

"I'm one of the palace physicians, the only female one. His Highness ordered that I attend to you personally," she said, her words ringing with pride.

It took Lauren a moment to realize who she meant. She was still a prisoner then, upgraded from that stark...*cell* to the sumptuous palace. "Well... *His Highness* can screw himself for all I care," she muttered, emotions batting at her from all directions.

The woman's mouth fell open, and she looked at Lauren as though she had grown two heads. Lauren felt like an ass. It wasn't really the woman's fault.

"I'm sorry...."

"Dr. Farrah Hasan."

"Dr. Hasan, I have to leave. In fact, if you can just hand me my phone." She pointed to her gray metallic handbag— the funky bag looked as out of place on the red velvet settee as she felt in the grandiose palace. "I'll call the airport and reschedule my flight."

"You can't leave, Ms. Hamby. Besides the fact that His Highness has forbidden it," she rushed over her words as if afraid that Lauren would lose it again, "given your condition, you're very weak. I recommend that you spend at least a week in bed and wait two weeks before you fly long-distance."

"My condition?" Lauren said, her heart beginning a strange thump-thump loud enough to reach her ears. "Nothing's wrong with me except the effects of dehydration." *Which was really His Highness's fault.* But she managed to keep the words to herself this time.

"Your pregnancy," Dr. Hasan said with a frown. "You're not aware of it?"

Lauren felt as if she'd been physically slapped. She shook her head, huffed a laugh at the ridiculousness of the suggestion. The doctor's eyes remained serious.

She couldn't be. "But that's not…"

She collapsed against the bed, shaking uncontrollably from head to toe. Her breaths became shaky, and a vicious churn started in her stomach. *Pregnant? How was that possible?* She took her pill without missing it a single day. She clutched the sheets with her hands, tears leaking out of the corner of her eyes.

Fear and shock vied with each other, a heaviness gathering in her belly.

She couldn't be pregnant. A child needed unconditional love, stability, two parents who loved it, who would put it before anything else, before their own ambitions and duties.

Zafir and she couldn't even bear to look at each other without distrust.

Panic unfurled its fangs, and she felt woozy again.

"Just breathe, Ms. Hamby," the doctor said, and Lauren let that crisp tone wash over her, glad to have someone tell her what to do.

As her breathing became normal again, a little flicker of something else crept in. She shoved her top away under the cotton sheets and splayed her fingers on her stomach.

A tiny life was breathing inside her, and it felt as though it breathed courage into her.

A baby.

Her job as an ER nurse at an inner-city hospital in Brooklyn consumed every ounce of her energy, both physical and emotional. Christ, she had never even had a normal boyfriend.

She saw and dealt with unwed, single mothers and their difficulties on a day-to-day to basis. That gritty reality coupled with her own childhood had made at least one thing clear in her head. She'd never wanted to bring a child into the world that couldn't have the love of both parents.

"Is everything okay with the...baby?" she said, her thoughts steering in another direction suddenly.

Dr. Hasan smiled, as though reassured of Lauren's mental state. "It is very early in the pregnancy, I'm assuming. As far your health, you're fine. But you're dehydrated and I suspect your iron content is low. Nothing that a week's rest and nutritious food wouldn't cure, though."

Lauren nodded, feeling a little calm. As much as she hated staying within a ten-mile radius of Zafir, she wasn't going to take any chances. She'd stay a week and then fly back to New York on her originally scheduled flight.

She needed to sort out her life, and she couldn't do that here. Once she was back in her own city, adjusted to this new change, then she would tell him.

"Are you friends with Zafir?"

Deep pride filled the doctor's eyes. "Yes, Zafir... I mean, *His Highness* and I have known each other since childhood."

So Farrah was not only his staff but one of his friends. A week was a long time surrounded by people who worshipped the ground Zafir walked on. "But as your patient, I have your discretion?"

She frowned. "Yes, of course, Ms. Hamby."

"Please call me Lauren." She tugged the sheet up and clasped her hands on top of it. "I need you to keep…*this,*" she said, as her fingers fluttered over her stomach, "between you and me, Dr. Hasan." A part of her flinched at the lie she was spouting with such little effort. "It doesn't concern Zafir and I would like to keep it that way."

A frown furrowed the doctor's forehead. "Of course, it's not something I will disclose to anyone. But if—"

Lauren turned away from her questions. It was better for everyone concerned if she said very little right then.

Zafir signed the last file with satisfaction and pushed it into the pile for his assistant. This was one of his pet projects, a plan sanctioning the money to upgrade the existing women's clinic on the outskirts of the city for the tribes that still resided in the desert and constantly faced the challenge of bringing their women into the city for medical care.

He stood up from the massive oak table and walked toward the liquor cabinet. He poured himself a glass of whiskey and drank it straight. It burned a fiery path through his throat and gut but did nothing to curb the seething mass of frustration. Knowing that Lauren was in the palace, just in reach, was messing with his self-control.

Tariq's death had put an end to their affair, but he had not forgotten the mindless pleasure he had found in her arms.

The man he was in Behraat couldn't have an affair without courting undue scrutiny from the High Council and more importantly, the wronged people of his country. He needed to create a different image, put distance between him and the scandalous life led by Tariq. Yet…

Arif stepped into his office, a tiny camcorder in his hand. "We found the man."

Zafir's heart pumped faster, as if he was on a stallion racing against a desert storm. "And?"

"He gave us the footage, said he didn't want to do anything to upset the balance of power in Behraat. As long as you give him an exclusive one-on-one."

Perversely, her friend's indifference toward Lauren's safety riled Zafir while she had refused to betray him in any way. "He did not inquire after Lauren?"

"He did. I took him to speak to the woman. He was satisfied about her safety and a little curious about her stay in the royal palace," Arif said, a little hint of his own dissatisfaction thrown in for good measure.

Excitement pulsed through Zafir. He pushed his chair back and stood up. "Say it, Arif."

"Send her away, immediately."

No other man would have dared to suggest what Arif had said. But his old mentor was nothing if not ruthlessly loyal to Behraat.

"Why?"

"That woman," Arif continued, showing his distaste by not mentioning Lauren by name, "is trouble. Only two days and she has already...unsettled you."

Zafir shook his head. "I walked away, in the middle of the night, without looking back. Hid my identity from her."

All he cared about now, or ever, was Behraat. Yet, the same thought plagued him. Did that mean he was not entitled to even the little pleasures he wanted?

"She's due a little anger."

His gaze steady, Arif shook his head. "You cannot let anything distract you from your path."

And what Arif didn't say was that he already had. Frustration and anger mixed in with a healthy dose of unsatisfied libido swirled through him.

All he had ever done was to give of himself to his father, even though he hadn't known it then, and to Behraat. And yet, in return, he would be denied such a small thing as the one woman that tempted him no end.

No!

"Should I live my life like a monk?" It was a question he'd already asked himself. And with Lauren within reach, the answer was becoming blurry to him.

"The best thing for your future, for the future of Behraat would be to find a suitable young woman, one who knows her place in your life and marry her. Cement your position in front of the High Council."

A pleasant, traditional, biddable Behraati woman would never talk back to him, would definitely not even think of striking him.

That's what the future held for him. But he was in no hurry to embrace it just yet.

Tariq's wife, Johara's portrait caught his attention.

Johara was delicate, stunningly beautiful, shy, the daughter of a member of a powerful High Council member. Someone like her was what he needed for a future wife.

Lauren, on the other hand, was the exact opposite of Johara. Tall and lithe, hardworking, tough, prickly, and unflinchingly honest.

She asked for nothing, made no demands of him, and had nearly killed herself with flu instead of asking for help once. She had few friends outside of her work at the inner-city ER, no personal life. They had been like two perfectly matched ships crossing each other at a port.

Yet she had come looking for him, had cared enough to mourn for him.

A dangerous temptation for a man who rarely allowed himself any personal attachments…

"My life is, always will be, about Behraat, Arif. No woman will change that. Or change me into something I never could be."

But, for once in his life, he wanted to indulge himself. She had made the choice to come, hadn't she? After the brutal reality of the past few weeks, maybe Lauren arriving in Behraat was his prize.

Just the thought of her was enough to tighten every muscle in his body with need.

But first, he needed to make it right with her. And he knew how to do just that.

After all, there had to be some perks to being the ruler of a nation.

Lauren pushed the French doors aside and stepped onto the private balcony. Dusk was an hour away and it painted the sky crimson. She tugged the edges of a cashmere sweater tighter around her shoulders, feeling the chill in the air.

It was something that amazed her even after a week in Behraat. As hot as it got during the day, with sunset, chill permeated the air.

She couldn't believe she was in the royal palace, home to the royalty of Behraat, with its various turrets and domes.

Landscaped gardens, water fountains, meandering pathways amid tiled courtyards, everywhere she looked, old-world charm, sheer opulence and unprecedented luxury greeted her. It was a setting straight out of a princess tale her aunt had read to her years ago from a book her parents had gifted her after another diplomatic stint in some far-off, exotic country, just like Behraat.

The quarters she'd been given boasted a large antique bed with the softest cotton sheets spun with threads of gold, satin drapes and the en suite bathroom with a marble bathtub was fit for a princess. Plush, colorful rugs snuggled against her bare feet, a vanity mirror framed with intricate gold filigree…everywhere she turned, the opulence of Zafir's wealth, the sheer differences in their worlds mocked her.

Even when she lay down on her bed, there was the soaring ceiling inlaid with an intricate mural that cast a golden glow over the room. As though she needed a reminder of where she was or who she was dealing with.

She turned around and walked back into the suite. Restlessness and uncertainty gnawed at her, even though it had been a full day since she had learned of her pregnancy. "You're a fully qualified doctor?" she shot at Farrah who hadn't left except for a couple of hours.

Farrah looked up from her journal and nodded.

"It doesn't bother you that he's ordered you to play nursemaid to me?"

"It's a small request from a man who saved me at my lowest without judgment, when…even my family had forsaken me." She put the journal aside. "And it is clear that you are important to him."

Lauren ignored the obvious question in Farrah's words and shot one of her own. "Because he has jailed me *here* rather than one of those underground cells?"

"You misunderstand. You're in Zafir's private wing. Women are not allowed here. If imprisoning you was what he intended, he could have put you anywhere." She paused as though waiting for the import of her words to sink in. "Here, he can be absolutely certain of your safety."

Lauren refused to attach any meaning to Farrah's revelation.

She walked toward the dark side table laden with exotic fruits and pastries. She picked up the elegant silver jug and poured sherbet into the gleaming silver tumbler and took a sip. Apparently, in Zafir's world, silverware meant actual *silverware*.

The smooth fruity liquid slid down her parched throat blissfully. "The only person posing a problem to my safety is *His Arrogant Highness*."

"There have been two attempts on his life since he returned to Behraat, Lauren."

The tumbler slid from Lauren's grasp, soundlessly spreading a stain on the thick Persian rug at her feet.

Lauren gripped the wooden surface, an image of Zafir dead instantly pressed upon her by her overactive mind. Nausea rose up through her, turning the sweet taste of the sherbet into bitterness.

That he might be dead was a reality she had accepted a few days ago. Yet having seen him, she couldn't bear the thought of anything happening to him. She picked up a napkin and knelt to soak up the stain from the rug. "Why would—"

A knock at the door to the suite cut off her question.

A woman, dressed in a maroon kaftan and head robes that covered her hair, entered the suite. She had a silver tray in her hand, the contents of it covered by a red velvet cloth lined with gold threads.

Kohl-rimmed eyes stole glances at her as the woman spoke to Farrah. Her eyes wide, Farrah stared at Lauren and back at the woman. "His Highness wants to see you in an hour on the rooftop garden," Farrah said, her gaze tellingly blank of any expression.

The woman stepped forward and stretched her arms. Lauren took a step back, unease settling low in her belly.

Her heart going thump-thump, she pulled the velvet cloth and bit back a gasp. With shaking hands, she took the precious emerald silk gown from the tray and unfolded it, the soft crunch of tissue wrapped in its folds puncturing the silence.

Thousands of tiny crystals, sewn along the demure neckline and the tight bodice, winked at her. A pencil line skirt flared from the waist with a knee-high slit in the back.

A dress fit for a princess, a sheikha, or a rich man's plaything.

It would fit her like a glove, Lauren realized. Her gaze caught Farrah's for a second, and the same knowledge lingered there. Her temper rising, she dropped the gown, feeling more dirty than she had ever felt.

The curiosity with which the two women watched her every move, every nuance in her expression, scraped at her nerves.

Were they coming to the same conclusion as her? A female *guest* tucked away in the High Sheikh's quarters, on whom he bestowed gifts of the most intimate kind.

What kind of a game was he playing?

A sick feeling coursed through Lauren, settling in her stomach. She showed the velvet case no such care as she had done the dress. She yanked it open and stared at its contents.

A diamond necklace, with matching earrings and bracelet. The name of the top designer in gold threading on the velvet case was redundant to Lauren. She knew this particular design too well. Tears that she dare not shed choked up her throat.

He remembered her obsession with diamonds.

Every surface in her apartment in Queens was littered with brochures and catalogs from the top diamond galleries of the world. It was her guilty pleasure to spend a lazy evening in her recliner, going through the catalogs, marking the ones she liked, while in reality, she didn't own a tiny pendant.

The diamonds glittered and winked at her as she closed the lid, struggling to keep a check on her unraveling temper.

Did he think she would be softened by this blatant display of wealth, that she would forget everything that had happened? That he could buy her off with expensive gifts?

The fact that he remembered her obsession plunged the stab of his betrayal a little deeper. Whatever he said now, whatever he did, she had to remember that he'd made the choice to cut her out of his life with little regret. That he'd suspected her of the worst.

She dropped the velvet case onto the tray on the bed. "Please instruct her to take it back, Farrah, and to inform His Highness that I don't intend to see him. Not today, not tomorrow, not ever again."

CHAPTER FOUR

LAUREN TIED THE sash on the plush thigh-length robe and walked into the sitting area of her suite. With another plush towel, she rubbed the wetness out of her hair. She would have lingered another hour in the marble tub, playing and luxuriating in the innumerable jets and settings, if she wasn't scared she would turn into a prune. "That marble tub is decadent, Farrah."

"I'm glad something in my palace gives you pleasure, Lauren."

Husky, honeyed—his tone sent waves of sensation rollicking over her already tingly flesh. Her knees wobbled. She pulled her towel off her face, her cheeks tightening with heat.

Uncurling himself from the velvet armchair, Zafir cut a direct path toward her, his gaze traveling over her with a thoroughness that instantly put her on edge. Flaring with shock, Farrah's gaze volleyed between them.

"Leave us, Farrah." He threw the command without turning his thoroughly disconcerting gaze from Lauren.

"I have nothing to say to you that Farrah can't—"

"I have," he said, stopping a few inches from her. Farrah had already gathered her things and quietly exited the room.

His hair still wet, he smelled so good that her stomach did a funny flip.

In a light brown V-neck T-shirt and tight blue jeans, he looked sexy and approachable. Like delicious dark chocolate that she wanted to sink her teeth into. The shirt exposed the strong column of his throat, hugged the hard contours of his chest and muscled abdomen.

Her throat dry, Lauren tucked her hands at her sides and tugged her gaze up.

His tawny gaze glinted with incinerating warmth, a hint of mockery in the grooves around his mouth. It swept over her with invasive familiarity, lingering far too long over the opening in her robe.

Her pulse went haywire, a new kind of oxygen deprivation drying her mouth now.

She tugged at the sash holding it together, the soft silk burning against her overheated skin. His hand shot out to her cheek in a quick movement, too fast for her hazy senses to grasp. Every cell in her being pushed her into leaning into his touch and she resisted it. Just.

When he touched her, his movements were gentle, tracing the circles she sported under her eyes. "You look awful." He said this in a tone that spoke of regret. As if it hadn't been in his power to not hurt her. As if he hadn't made that choice himself.

She stepped back. "Thanks for noticing, *Your Highness*, and for deigning to see me," she drawled. "I should curtsy, but seeing that you had me locked up here for two days, I'm not in the mood. Instruct your staff to release me. I want to leave, at once."

A frown twisted his brows and then smoothed down. Her hands instantly went to her midriff and that incisive gaze followed. She pretended to secure the knot of her robe, her fingers shaking. Heat flushed her from within when he moved closer again, triggering every nerve into a hyper-aware state, stealing rational thought.

"Stop that," she said softly, suddenly wishing the dark stranger from that afternoon back. She wanted to be angry with him, *she was*, yet her body seemed disjointed from her mind.

He raised his hands like shields, a butter-won't-melt expression on his face. "Stop what?"

"Looking at me like that," she croaked.

"It gives me pleasure to look at you."

She rolled her eyes, hoping that he couldn't hear the thudding of her heart. "I fell for that line six weeks ago. Fool me once—"

His finger on her lips cut her off. She trembled all over, the simple contact breathing a firestorm of need all over. "Choosing that gown and the jewelry was the most pleasure I've had in six weeks."

He had picked the gown himself? Her heart, if possible, skipped a beat, his words falling over her like sparkly, magic dust, ensnaring her senses into a web of intoxicated desire. How else could she explain the gooey mass in the center of her stomach?

"If you had worn it and accepted my invitation for dinner, I would have been even more pleased."

"*I...me...my pleasure,* self-absorbed much, Zafir?" she mocked him. Something uncoiled in his gaze but her bitter words were the only things she had to fight him with. "Your gifts don't mean anything to me except that you think you can buy your way out of anything. You locked me up here. Dinner with you is the last thing I want."

"I wanted to make sure Farrah could take proper care of you. What is bothering you?" he said, steel creeping into his words.

"You're kidding, right? Should I fall at your feet because you moved me here, because you threw some gifts at me? Three days ago, you accused me of conspiring against you and now..." She vibrated with anger and hurt, barely getting words out. "You talk to me as if nothing happened. I've had quite enough of you and this...place."

"I would like to apologize for that. I knew that you weren't capable of scheming like that."

"And you came to this realization after getting concrete proof from David and not a second before?"

His mouth hardened and Lauren realized she hated this version of him. Every time he spoke or thought of Behraat, he became someone she didn't know, someone she didn't want to know. "I needed that video, Lauren. I have to be ruthless from time to time. Consider it one of the hazards of being the ruler."

"More like the effect of being drunk on your own power."

Instead of the anger she had expected, his mouth curved into a smile. His gaze moved to her mouth and she felt his perusal like a tingle. "Surrounded by my people, I've forgotten how outspoken you are." He pushed a lock of hair from her forehead. "It was the first thing I noticed about you."

Whatever she had been about to say flitted away. Pure sensation skittered over her skin. He cupped her jaw and pulled her close, the rough pad of his thumb rubbing her skin. "I brought Huma to the ER, you took one look at her, and demanded if I was the one who had given her those bruises. The way you looked at me with fire burning in your eyes…" His Adam's apple bobbed up and down.

"You reminded me of a lioness I once saw in the zoo… ferocious and breathtaking." His tone became molten, honeyed on those last words, a fire burning in his eyes.

"I have never in my life become so hard just by looking at a woman, *ya habeebti*."

Wet warmth pooled at her core and she clutched her thighs together.

Torture, that's what it was. And worse than being locked up. Because when he accused her of nefarious intentions, she could fight him, and despise him.

But when he spoke like that, with desire, with honesty, with nothing but that warmth, she stood no chance.

She tried to let her body go slack, but she had no control over her own muscles. All she wanted was to drop the robe and let him ease the ache between her legs. *God,* and he would…with those clever fingers, he would unravel so easily and efficiently…until there was only her and him and that fire between them.

"Stop touching me," she finally managed, sounding breathless and shivery.

Forcing her back until the back of her legs hit the bed, he crowded her. His thumb moved over her lower lip, the heat from his body swathing her. "You love it when I touch you. In fact, while we were together, we couldn't get enough of each other."

"I used to." She somehow pulled her sanity together finally. "Now all I want is to put several thousand miles between us."

His gaze became hard, a muscle jumping in his jaw. "I thought you would have cooled off by now." He spread his hands around, and the lack of economy in that movement betrayed his rising temper that his even tone hid. "Seeing that you assumed I was dead and I'm clearly not, I thought you would get over your shock and be happy to see me."

"And that we would take up where we left off six weeks ago?" she yelled the words, masking the lump in her throat. The incredible arrogance in his assumption left her shaking, dousing her desire with the efficiency of an ice-cold bath. "I'm never going to get over it, Zafir.

"If I weren't a…*sentimental fool* who jumped on a plane, we wouldn't have seen each other again…*ever.* You made a deliberate choice to walk out of my life that night. Don't act as though you care now."

Her legs quaked beneath her when she meant to move away from him. She felt light-headed.

His arms forming a steel cage, Zafir picked her up instantly and laid her down on the settee. His forehead wreathed in concern as he studied her face. "*Ya Allah*, you were about to faint again. What the hell is going on with you, Lauren?"

She had let herself get upset by his gifts this morning and barely touched her lunch. No wonder she felt so weak, so vulnerable. She couldn't do this again and again. She couldn't let her child pay the price for her weakness.

Moving back on the chaise, she wrapped her hands around her legs. "I'm just hungry," she whispered. He immediately picked up the intercom and ordered enough food to feed an army.

When he reached for her, she shook her head. "Leave, before the staff arrives."

"Why?"

"Because you've already given them enough to gossip about. I would like to not become another dirty spectacle of your palace, Zafir."

His jaw tight, he glared at her. "You are awful at taking care of yourself. I will wait until I'm sure you're not going to collapse again," he said, the frustrated anger in his voice snaring her again.

After everything that had happened that day, it was the last thing she wanted to hear. "What the hell is that supposed to mean?"

"You had the most virulent flu two weeks before I left, remember? And it's obvious you've not recovered from it. When Huma found you on the bathroom floor and called me, you looked like you were about to die. I literally carried you to the clinic. And here you are again looking like a ghost. What have you been doing, starving yourself?"

Shying her gaze away from him, Lauren drank a glass of ice-cold water.

She had been worried over *him*. But there was no point in reiterating what a fool she had been.

Instead, her thoughts moved to that evening he had taken her to the clinic. For a week, he and Huma had taken shifts, nursing her back to health, not leaving her alone even for a few minutes. By the time her friend Alicia had heard about her illness and arrived with chicken soup, Lauren had been halfway to recovering.

And when she had gotten better, he had come to her that evening, and dismissed Huma, a wild light in his eyes…

It was the last time she had seen him, the only time he had actually stayed over at her apartment in two months…

Her gaze flew open, her stomach twisting at the final nail in the coffin.

Zafir laid his hand on her forehead, frowning. "Do you feel faint again?"

She shook her head, dislodging his hand. "Huma knew, didn't she?"

A stillness crept into his face. "Knew what?"

"She knew about us…that we were…" she forced the words out, killing any tender thought she had ever indulged in, "having sex?"

His expression became distasteful. "I do not discuss my sex life with Huma. But yes."

"Did she also know you were leaving the next morning?"

He looked as though he was weighing his response and she wondered why when he had given her the absolute truth earlier. "Huma's the daughter of an old friend whose life was in danger here. She was under my care in New York. I had to tell her that I was leaving, that I had made plans for her."

Huma had left a week after he had. With a hug and something muttered in Arabic that Lauren couldn't understand to her question about Zafir.

"Did she tell you that I had been worried?"

"Yes."

She bolted from the chaise, fury finally, *mercifully* coming to her rescue. All this could have been avoided. It could have all ended in New York just as he'd intended.

She turned back to him, one last question gnawing at her gut.

Leave it alone, Lauren, a part of her whispered, the part that preferred to cling to delusion.

No.

Knowing the bitter, eviscerating truth was better than driving herself crazy for years to come with speculation. She'd learned early on, with her parents' indifference, that hope was toxic, gnawing away at one's self.

"Were you *ever* going to call, Zafir?"

Silence stretched between them, its cruel fingers shredding her patched up nerves.

"Leave," she whispered.

He turned her around, his fingers gripping her tight. "It was a decision I made. But I did…*regret* the necessity of making it. It doesn't mean I didn't think about you in these last few weeks." Arrogant features softened. "Stay in Behraat for a while, as my guest."

She stared at him, her mouth hanging open for several seconds. They were mere words but she could already feel herself softening, traitorous desire whispering sweet temptations in her ears.

It seemed nothing had changed in how she reacted to his magnetic presence. After everything she had gone through in the past few weeks, she was ashamed to feel the thrum of excitement his words incited.

"No," she forced the word out.

He trapped her again. Rock-hard thighs pressed into hers. Molten gaze hovered over her mouth and a low hum began to vibrate over her skin. "Why not?"

She licked her lips and straightened, fisting her hands. It was either that or touch him. God, how she wanted to run her fingers over his sensual mouth, lean into him and relish the heat of his body.

His hands crept into her hair and tugged her closer, his long fingers encircling her nape. Awareness shot through her like a surge of current. "You're a workaholic and haven't taken a vacation in forever. Besides, I've missed our Friday, what did you call them, *movie and...make out sessions*."

"You're serious?" she said.

He didn't answer her question, only pulled her closer. It went straight to her head, making her light-headed with longing, shooting need to the apex of her thighs, drenching her in liquid heat.

How she wanted to close her eyes and let him take her to ecstasy once again. How she wanted to delude herself that physical pleasure was intimacy...that lust was caring...that she mattered and not just as a willing woman.

Fears and insecurities she had repressed for so long festered in that void. And she detested herself for feeling so much. "I can't. In fact, if I never lay eyes on you again after tonight, it'll be too soon for me."

A vein fluttered at his temple, his grip tight in her hair. Her pulse hammered, her insides feeling as though she had taken a vertical leap.

"You're a liar." His mouth hovered mere inches from her, his breath brushed her skin in a featherlight touch, teasing. "Do you have any idea how I long to possess you again? How much I need you, Lauren?" His gaze came alive, his words low and husky. "And if I kiss your luscious mouth, can you honestly say you'll stop me? Can you deny us both the pleasure we want so much?"

Lauren shook her head, knowing everything she felt was reflected in her eyes. A grim satisfaction shadowed over his face, its razor edge mocking her feeble defenses.

"No. I'll admit that I'll enjoy the sex as much as you do.

I'll go as far as to say you're the best lay I've ever had," she said, hungry to see his smooth charade fracture.

Thunder danced in his gaze, his razor-sharp cheekbones streaked with color. Even as he knew that she had had one lover before him, a boyfriend in college who had been more into his military career than into her.

"The best lay you've ever had?" he inquired silkily, the force of his anger all the more fierce for the leash with which he reined it.

"Yes," she said, tilting her chin up with a recklessness she was far from feeling. "You're extremely skilled and generous when it comes to sex."

Reducing their affair to the crudest terms was the only thing that would save her. From him and herself.

"But I have to resist the attraction, the lure of self-delusion this time. Your power and the ruthlessness with which you wield it, the reckless indifference it affords you of other's feelings, especially someone like me who's all too willing to fall into your bed…

"How long before you decide that you've had enough of me, before you decide I don't belong in your world? How long before, once again, you walk out of my bed in the middle of the night and have one of your guards throw me out without so much as a goodbye?"

An immense stillness came over him. Her breath hitching in her throat, Lauren waited. For something—for refusal, for anger, anything that refuted her accusation.

But nothing came.

His silence plunged her deep into a vortex of painful memories.

Discarded in the name of ambition and lofty goals, picked back up with no thought to her feelings, and discarded again. She couldn't count the number of times her parents had hurt her.

The insecurity, the fear that she didn't somehow measure up, her resolution to make no demands—a vicious circle of pain that stole every ounce of joy from her. That's what she would bring upon herself if she succumbed.

Stepping back from him when every inch of her thrummed to be with him, it was the hardest thing she had ever done.

Her heart stuttered anew at the dark beauty of the man.

God, he was the father of her child, the first man who had made her feel so much…the first man for whom she had forgotten herself. And she…she had to walk away.

"If you truly respect me, leave now, Zafir. Let me leave Behraat."

Even now, a fragment of hope flickered inside her, waiting for him to persuade her otherwise.

He stepped back, slowly, irrevocably and Lauren's knees gave out under her.

"As you wish, Lauren." That dark gaze swept over her face with a thoroughly hungry appraisal before he turned and marched out of the suite.

Without looking back once.

Lauren sank against the bed, struggling to pull air into her lungs, squeezing her eyes to keep the wet heat at bay.

She would never amount to more than a willing woman to Zafir. And maybe she had been okay with that status quo in New York, but not anymore.

Not when it was her child's well-being in question.

A playful giggle echoed somewhere and she turned toward the balcony looking out onto the vast courtyard below. A boy, somewhere between five and nine—she couldn't tell any closer than that—ran on the cobbled stones, his dark hair shining under the light of bronze torches, a mischievous smile on his face, chased by a man around the fountain.

The man let him run around two more circles before he caught up with him and slung him on his shoulder.

She felt as if a fist was squeezing her heart as she realized the magnitude of her decision.

Zafir was the ruler of a nation, a man who had a long list of priorities in which she didn't feature, a man who could set aside everything else quite ruthlessly when it came to Behraat. And she and her child would only be complications in that path.

After what she had suffered at her parents' hands, she would never put her child through it.

It had been the longest week of Lauren's life. She felt as though she was sitting on shifting sands with no tether.

More than once, she had picked up the phone, eager to blurt out the news to Zafir. She just wasn't programmed to lie or hide the truth as she was doing.

Zafir refused to let her go back to the hotel, so she spent her days locked up in the palace. Scared of weakening, she cut herself off from everything. And when life intruded, it only brought a truth that crystallized her decision.

Having learned that Lauren was the sheikh's *scandalous female guest*, Huma had come calling. Hugged Lauren and chattered on and on about how decent life was in Behraat now, about how she had enrolled herself in a women's college to study nursing.

"Just like you," Huma had whispered with a proud smile.

And in the same innocent way she did everything else, she informed Lauren of the rumors about the sheikh's upcoming wedding and the celebrations that would ensue.

Nausea filled her throat as Huma continued merrily.

Childhood friends, reunited after several years, daughter of a High Council member, born to be a sheikha and so on...

The excruciating doubts she had had about hiding the

pregnancy from him, the conflict that had eroded her from within, everything evaporated at the bitter news.

Not even a little regret pricked her as she packed that night.

Her child would be secondary to neither duty nor a new bride in his father's life. She would make sure of that.

CHAPTER FIVE

LAUREN STARED AROUND the terminal, the beautiful archi-tecture of the private airport building filling her with awe. The same soaring circular ceilings, grand archways and a colorfully hued marble stretched as far as she could see, a far cry from the commercial airport she and David had flown into.

On learning that she'd been scheduled on a privately chartered flight, Lauren had called it a huge wastage of resources. But as Farrah had pointed out with a lingering question in her eyes, the sheikh had decreed that she be sent off in style.

And no one could defy the mighty sheikh's word.

Whose withdrawal had been absolute and chilling.

When her stomach grumbled, Lauren opened her en-ergy bar and took a bite. After the elaborate, mouthwater-ing meals of the past week, the granola bar tasted foul in her mouth but she forced herself to chew.

"We're ready to board you," announced the flight atten-dant, carefully shying away his gaze from Lauren.

From gleaming dark wood paneling to supple wide leather seats sitting on priceless Persian rugs constituted the decor. A flat-screen plasma television faced the seats.

Despite the disparity in their lifestyles and cultures, there had been a connection between them from the first moment. A connection that now had a permanent conse-quence...

Her throat felt thick with an emotion she refused to name.

A woman, dressed in traditional tunic and trousers with her hair concealed in a loose scarf, approached her, a glass of sparkling water in her hand. "Hello, Ms. Hamby," she said deferentially. "I'm a qualified nurse, so please let me know if you feel faint."

Had he informed his whole staff that she was incapable of looking after herself? "I'm a nurse too, so I would know," she added a little sharply.

Sighing, Lauren peered through the window and saw the jagged outline of the capital city set against sprawling desert land in the distance. Turreted domes and spires stood out against the sky and she hungrily clutched the sight to herself.

"Aren't you leaving?" she asked the woman.

"I accompany you to New York," she said demurely, "and then, return to Behraat."

Lauren set her glass on the table so fast that the cold water spilled on her fingers.

This was going too far. She'd decided to tolerate the jet because she didn't want to draw Zafir's attention by complaining about it. But she drew the line at wasting a qualified nurse's time.

She had learned from Farrah that women qualified in the medical field were just not enough for the growing demand in the outlying villages of the city where families still refused to let the women see male doctors.

"Please ask whoever's in charge to take me back to the commercial airport."

"But the sheikh himself—"

"If he has a problem with this," Lauren replied, as she stood up and grabbed her handbag, "he can come see me himself."

The woman gasped.

"You have your wish, *habeebti*," came the sudden, soft reply behind her.

Lauren whirled so fast that she was dizzy.

Zafir. The sheer force of his presence was like a blast of toe-curling heat. Her insides plummeted alarmingly.

"You're also going to wish," his tone was silky smooth, like velvet cloaking a knife's edge as he dismissed the nurse with a flick of his head, "we had never met by the time I'm through with you."

With that veiled threat, he threw a file at her. The contents scattered with a soft whisper that nevertheless felt like a thudding roar. As though even the flimsy paper didn't dare disobey his command, a sheet flew toward her.

Goose bumps broke out on her skin. She didn't need to read the paper to know what it said. The red file with her name in capital letters, the small insignia, the seal of the palace physician, was enough.

"Tongue-tied, Lauren?"

Now his voice rang with power, cold ferocity, absolute disgust. Her stomach churned fiercely, her heart racing far too fast and far too loud.

He knew. God, he knew, and he looked so angry. Why? Why was he so angry?

She picked up the papers from the floor, one by one, her movements slow and shaky, her thoughts in a whirl. Slowly, she stood up and faced him.

A white cotton tunic with a Nehru collar hung carelessly over his broad chest, dark hair on golden brown skin peeking through its opening. The very unassuming, casual way of his dressing only served to emphasize how easily he wore his power.

Molten heat uncoiled low in her belly, as instinctual as her breathing.

He gripped her elbow and pulled her toward him. "Explain that file."

Was his fury because of the truth she had hidden or the

fact that she had dared to? Was that a shadow of hurt beneath his anger?

Doubts piled upon her, weakening her. His nearness wrecked her balance, her mind, compelling little pinpricks of guilt.

No, it had been the hardest decision she'd ever made in her life.

She looked into the sharp planes of his aristocratic face, forced herself to keep her tone light—a herculean task with his gaze peeling layers off her. "It goes something like this. A man and a woman have fantastic, mind-blowing sex thinking they are protected by her pill, but the pill fails because the woman is on antibiotics, *annndd...*" she made a singsong sound, her throat drying up at the lick of molten fury in his gaze, turning the tawny irises to scorching flames "...a few weeks later, the woman is pregnant. Your basic biology in action."

A curse fell from his mouth—something she had no hope of understanding except that it was nasty and aimed at her, his long fingers digging into her arm.

"Learn to curb that tongue of yours, *ya habeebti*, or I'll put it to a more pleasurable activity next time."

Something hot and twisty and unbearably achy gripped her lower belly, her cheeks burning up. Their gazes met and held, his meaning clear in the dark heat in it. "I'm not going to acknowledge that with a refusal."

He laughed then and while it etched gorgeous grooves into his cheeks, it lacked any warmth. The luxurious cabin felt chilly. "You think I cannot command you to do my bidding, Lauren? All that lacked until now was intention on my behalf."

"You're trying to frighten me."

"Try me then, *habeebti*. Try and see how far I can go when I'm pushed, when I'm denied what's mine."

She swallowed and took a deep breath. Angering him

was not, had never been, her objective. "How did you find out? Did—"

"No, the dedicated doctor that she is, Farrah kept her silence and faces my wrath."

Her heart sank to her toes. "I told her this had nothing to do with you, Zafir. Don't punish her because you're angry with me."

"Worry about your own fate."

Beating down the fear that swamped her, she tried to be rational. "I don't understand your reaction, Zafir."

"No? Then let me explain it to you. You found out that you were pregnant *with my child,* and decided to flee Behraat without a word." He ran a shaky hand over his face, the starkness of the gesture contrasting sharply with the fury in his words. "And to think I was honoring your wish, that I was being respectful… How dare you hide something so important from me?"

Something so important. Was it?

Suddenly she had springboarded into a category that merited his precious time and attention? That more than anything pierced her, robbing her of her innate decency, turned her bloodthirsty. "Are you so sure that it is yours then, Zafir?"

An icy mask fell over his face, and he loosened his grip on her and thrust her back from him with infinite care. He studied her with a detached coldness that turned the blood in her veins into ice. "No, I don't know that, do I?"

Plucking the phone from the wall, he barked a command to be connected to Farrah. Ordered a DNA test and slammed the handset into the wall without waiting for a response. It dangled by the cord, back and forth, the rubbery sound of it reverberating in the silence.

Lauren gripped her forehead, all fight deflating out of her. She had pushed him until the veneer of his civility was ripped at her feet. She had no one to blame except herself.

And she wondered, with an instinct she didn't understand if she had hurt him with her callous words.

Her throat was like sandpaper when she spoke. "It is yours, Zafir."

His back to her, he remained dangerously silent.

Despite all the disappointments she'd faced, she had never been a spiteful person. She hadn't intended her departure as a malicious move. She simply refused to let her child endure the same uncertainty, the same gut-wrenching pain of learning that he or she didn't feature highly in its parents' life.

"It's not possible to perform a DNA test so soon in the pregnancy," she whispered. "I will get one done as soon as it is safe and send you the results."

When he turned and looked down at her, she realized she was pathetic, imagining things that weren't possible, still so weak where he was concerned.

Because there was no hurt in his gaze. A smile, if the cruel curve of his mouth could be called that, bared his teeth, the triumphant light in his stance letting butterflies loose into her stomach.

Cold calculation glinted in his gaze, as though he was devising ways to punish her and having fun while doing it. "You're not going anywhere, not until you give birth to my child. After that, you can disappear into the sands of the desert for all I care."

Zafir watched as Lauren paled, held his gaze defiantly, realized he was serious and then fell back into her seat with a soft thud.

Instinct and something else, something shameful and useless and weakening like honor maybe, something the *great Rashid Al Masood* had taught him when he had been a boy, kicked in, and he found himself shooting out of his seat to help her.

No.

He shoved away the chivalry, crushed the very code of honor he had embraced early in his life after hearing whispered taunts about his parentage.

He'd always been discreet about how he'd indulged his lust, had cautiously distanced himself from Tariq and his wild, orgiastic parties.

All because he had been determined to not be the cause of some woman's distress.

The only time he had weakened, the only time he had forgotten that he could never let any personal attachment distract him was with Lauren. And her betrayal plunged the dagger the deepest because he had thought her above it.

If she had left, if she had disappeared...he would be unaware of the existence of his child. Just as he hadn't known of his parentage until just a few years back.

She tucked herself into the leather seat, retreating as far back as possible, *as though she didn't trust him.* The irony of it would have amused him if he wasn't seething with the need to punish her.

And he knew how to punish that independent, strong mind of hers, knew her weakness. An insidious thrill shot through him, cooling the edge of his anger.

"You're bluffing," she finally said, trying for defiance but failing.

He stretched his legs, settled into the seat opposite her and took his own sweet time answering.

Let her stew in fear, he thought with a bitterness that spread like an infection. Let her wonder what the powerful, arrogant sheikh would do with her now.

He had her where he wanted, he realized, excitement pulsing in his blood. And there was a freedom in knowing that she was like any other woman.

"Try to leave Behraat and see."

Little beads of moisture pearled over her upper lip, despite the air-conditioning.

"You're angry, I get that. But consider reality, Zafir. We're talking about a child here. You can't decide you want it now and then put it away when *something more important* comes along."

"You dare to preach to me of the intricacies of parenthood? Let us not delude ourselves of what this is really about.

"The fact that I walked away from you. I didn't pander to what you wanted, so you pay me back by robbing me of my child."

"It. Is. Not," she whispered, her long legs uncoiling from under her. "I was furious with you, yes, but I've accepted that our...*relationship* meant nothing to you. I—"

"Your actions speak otherwise." He moved toward her, his mind reeling with infinite questions. "What would you have told my child? That his father didn't want her or him, that he rejected him?"

She bolted from the seat, her arms around her midriff, her breasts rising and falling. "I would never lie to my child."

"Only its father then."

"I didn't lie to you. And I... I would have let you know eventually."

"*Eventually*?" He shot up from the seat, his temper seething again. "It was not your decision to make."

Her lithe form bristling with emotion, she poked him in the chest. "You're accusing me? You're the ruler of a nation, Zafir.

"You ruthlessly bury anything if it clashes with your rule. Can you blame me in thinking this baby would only be an unwanted complication? That its well-being, even its mere existence would be so far down the list for a man whose first priority will always be Behraat, a man who's on the verge of getting married to another woman?"

A smile teased the edges of his mouth, and he let it.

He took another step forward, forcing her to step back until her back hit the wood-paneled wall of the craft. He slapped his palms on either side of her, his gaze dropping to her mouth. She bristled with energy yet her breath was slow, chunky.

Striking flame to oil, that's what it would be if he touched her. That's what it had been from the second he had laid eyes on her.

"Now I see how your mind works. You heard rumors about my wedding and thought '*here he is propositioning me and getting ready to marry another woman*'?

"So I'll rob him of the knowledge of his child. You pride yourself on being a smart, educated woman, yes? Didn't it occur to you to talk to me once?"

Her breathing becoming raspier. "This was not payback, Zafir."

"No? Although in a twisted way, it shows that you were jealous at the thought of my wedding."

Something very much like a growl erupted from her. Her hands fell to his chest, fisted tight and pushed him back. He tucked them into his own and held his footing, her knuckles digging into his palms. "I've no desire to feature in a man's life for whom my only value is the pleasure I can provide in his bed. One who will discard me at a whim."

Tension turned those high cheekbones into tight angles, her mouth quivering and fighting.

"I've been lied to, dropped off like a pet at a relative's door, got picked up for a summer, got dropped off again by my own parents so many times in the name of duty, ambition and whatnot. I don't want my child to feel like that, okay?

"I won't allow you to do that.

"Will he or she ever come first with you, Zafir? Over anything else, over Behraat, over your precious duty? Because that's what this child means to me."

He stilled, her words striking him like a whip.

She was right. A child deserved better than lies and excuses, better than being used as a pawn. His own childhood had been a lie and he couldn't tolerate it.

He wanted to brush her concerns away, but the stark pain in her gaze wouldn't let him. "Whatever else I'm unable to give this child, it will know that I love it. And I will use everything within my power before I let you corrupt its mind against me."

Lauren swayed at the coldness of Zafir's threat.

His resentment was like a force field she couldn't penetrate. His anger, she was beginning to understand barely, but there was a glimmer of pain in it that disconcerted her. "If you care about the welfare of the baby, then let me go, Zafir. I would never deny your rights."

"No," he said, his voice raised enough to reverberate around them. "Get this into your mind, Lauren, for once and for all. I will never let a child of mine grow up without knowing me," he said, "nor will I agree to be a stranger who lives a million miles away."

She slackened against the wall. "Then we have a problem."

"I do not see one."

Her stomach tightened into a knot. He was too calm, too sure of his own mind, which sent panic rippling along her nerves. "I live in New York, you live here. I'd call that a *major* problem."

"Your life in New York is over."

His will was like an immovable, invisible wall. And still, she tried to bang away at it, because the alternative was unthinkable. "You can't dictate what my life is, force me to turn it upside down. I'm not one of your minions."

His gaze became hard, his tone relentlessly resolute. "If you want to be a mother to my child, you do it in Behraat."

"You've got to be…" But no, he was not joking. Lauren's gut knotted so hard she couldn't speak for a few seconds. "I don't see you prepared to give up anything. How about it, Zafir?"

He smiled, the bitterness in it sharp enough to cut her.

She could see the axis of her world tilting, every preconception she'd ever harbored about Zafir crushed by the autocratic man in front of her. There was nothing civil or kind about him anymore.

There was nothing but a chilling frost.

"Can you give the baby the best care by yourself in New York, living in that little dingy studio while working night shifts six days a week? You have no family to help and your friends…other single women who work just as hard as you do.

"Who will watch the baby while you work round-the-clock shifts? Who will help you when you walk in the door barely able to stand on your own feet?"

His words rang with logic, piercing holes in her plans, shredding her armor to pieces. "And if I don't agree?"

He shrugged and she fisted her hands, filled with the urge to hit him, to do anything to shake that cold mask so strong that it frightened her. "Then you will be free to leave Behraat once you give birth, to your hassle-free life."

His gaze moved to her midriff, and she hugged herself tighter. "My child will have everything it requires except a mother. And who knows? It's even possible that it might be better off without its deceitful mother. What is the guarantee that you will be a good one?"

Her shoulders shook, bile rose through her. She swallowed to push it back, to hold back the scream clawing its way up her throat. And yet, he stood there, staring at her, no concern or any other emotion in those golden eyes, the true man behind the stranger she'd known in New York. "You're doing this to punish me."

"You decided to leave without giving me a choice, but I'm generous. It's your choice whether you want to be a part of the baby's life."

"That's not a choice, that's an ultimatum."

"No, Lauren. My decision would have been the same had you come to me." There was a resigned finality to his tone. "Our child would have had two parents who respected each other, trusted each other. You would have had a say in the child's future. Now, you're only a glorified babysitter. I will never again trust you.

"How I intend to punish you…"

That voice became molten honey, naked hunger dancing in his gaze as it slowly flitted to her mouth. To her eternal shame, she felt it like an incinerating spark all across her skin.

No, God, no, she screamed inside her head, struggling to control her skittered breath, her tightening cheeks. *Hate him, resist him*, she begged of herself.

If her body was ever going to let go of the strange hold he had on it, it would be this moment.

Instead, amid the growing panic and helplessness that surged within her, heat and need vied viciously for space. So she latched on to the one thing that perversely grounded her. "You despise me, I see it shining in your eyes."

He tilted that powerful frame forward and the tips of her breasts grazed his hard chest. Need knotted her nipples and she whimpered. Half entreaty, half retreat. "I can see the loathing for me in your eyes, too." His hoarse voice caressed the rim of her ear. "But if I run my hand over—"

She slammed her palm over his mouth and then he was

whispering into her skin, his words a searing promise. "This time, I'm going to take what I want, Lauren."

Self-loathing lent her courage she wouldn't have had otherwise. "An experienced, disposable mistress on the side while you take a biddable, virginal wife and spawn heirs for your great country?"

He laughed, the tendons in his neck stretching with the movement. But something moved in the glittering depths of his eyes. Loathing? Fear? "That would complete your picture of me as a monster and justify your own appalling actions, yes?"

"I won't be willing this time, Zafir."

His hand curling around her nape, he pulled her closer. Languorous heat exploded as he whispered the words at the corner of her mouth. "I shall ensure you surrender that very will and I shall enjoy taking it from you."

A soundless scream left her mouth, a sliver snaking down Lauren's spine. Even then, instead of protest, she said "And then?"

"And then, it's only a matter of time before the fire between us burns out." Resignation danced in his gaze as he stepped back from her. "You will be one of the ex-mistresses of the Sheikh of Behraat, languishing somewhere in the palace and the woman who bore his first child."

For days after he had left Lauren at the airstrip—barely containing his ragged temper, because he was sure, for all his threats, he would have despised himself for the rest of his life if he had taken her right there while he turned into exactly the monster she thought him to be—he hadn't been able to concentrate on any of the numerous tasks awaiting his attention.

"It is yours, Zafir."

Much as he despised what she had intended, he didn't need a DNA test to know she spoke truth.

Once he had acknowledged that beneath his simmering anger came the realization that ate away at him—mind and heart and soul.

His child would be a bastard, just like him, if he didn't marry her.

His child would question his place in society, in the royal hierarchy, would know that keening gnawing of rejection, just like Zafir had known for years.

At his desk, he opened the file Farrah had given him that morning and looked at the pregnancy report.

Lauren would hate it, he knew instinctively, to be tied to him. She would hate a life of traditions and customs, hate the curbed freedom in the spotlight and personal sacrifices. The depth of her pain about her childhood had been a revelation in so many ways.

She would hate to bend to his will in and out of the bedroom, taking a third or fourth or tenth place in his life, to limit herself to the narrow confines of being his wife, the mother of his children.

Because Lauren demanded just as fiercely as she gave, something he should have realized long ago.

What stunned him to the depth of his core was how perversely amenable he was to the idea of making her his wife, of conquering that infuriatingly strong will of hers, of reveling in her thrilling sexuality night after night, of having someone in his life whose passions and strength and will ran as deep as his.

But he was not just Zafir.

He was Zafir Al Masood.

With the High Council still bitter about his rule and the perceived instability of the royal house in the minds of his people, Lauren was the last woman he could marry, the worst choice for his sheikha.

Which meant his child would be born out of wedlock

and face everything it ensued. Just as he had because his mother had been his father's mistress.

With a growl that ripped out of him, he grabbed the priceless, gold-embossed seal of generations of Al Masoods and threw it at the wall.

The weight of Behraat pressed at him from all sides. For a man who was supposed to be powerful, at that moment he felt anything but.

His life was not his own. It had never been.

CHAPTER SIX

LAUREN DIDN'T SEE Zafir again over the next three weeks.

Only a hazy recollection remained of how she had arrived at the palace again.

His ruthless words, the press of those hard thighs against hers, the caressing heat of his words against her skin…*that* she remembered with a vivid intensity and with an alarming frequency.

Maybe if she had something to do other than being his pampered, very pregnant captive. Even her leave of absence at the clinic had been handled with super efficiency at the request of the sheikh's administrative office.

She had never been so well looked after, not even when she had been a child.

There was a woman whose primary duty was to help her bathe—a fact she had learned when *said woman* had walked into the bath one day while Lauren was lounging in the tub, after which Lauren never forgot to lock the door behind her—a personal chef and a nutritionist who stopped by every morning asking after her appetite, a yoga instructor—which Farrah had informed her had been difficult to find, but Zafir remembered that she did yoga—and then, there was Farrah checking on her every evening, though she always seemed exhausted.

And even with the very minimal understanding she was trying to gain of Arabic—because her child was going to be half Arab—she grasped one thing.

They all knew that she was carrying the child of the High Sheikh of Behraat. The numerous staff that waited

on her hand and foot was perfectly courteous, but she saw
the curiosity in their eyes. Caught the word *Nikah* ban-
died about.

When she'd realized it meant wedding, which painted
an image of Zafir with a young, biddable bride, it felt as if
her heart would be ripped out of her chest. Until she realized what the staff *was* speculating about.

Lauren was carrying the sheikh's child but there was
to be no wedding. Because, *of course,* a Westerner like
her could never be a proper sheikha. She was only suitable for one thing.

"This time, I will take what I want."

Those words haunted her in the pitch-dark of the night
when she lay in her luxurious bed, restless in her overheated skin. When she couldn't lie to herself anymore.
When she admitted that, if he came to her, if his powerfully
naked body joined her on the cool sheets, that compelling
gaze captivating hers, she would beg him for his wicked
words, his rough hands, his utter possession.

But the glimpse of pain before he had become cruelly
cold again—it haunted her, made her curious about him.

Her only source, however, was Farrah, who had be-
grudgingly begun uttering monosyllabic responses to Lauren's questions, a vast improvement over the glares and
silent nods of the past two weeks.

Lauren took the bull by the horns as Farrah checked her
pulse. "How long will you be angry with me?"

Farrah sighed, her forehead creased in a delicate frown.
"It was your decision to make. But I failed Zafir. I've
known him all my life, I know what he…" She studied
Lauren, weighing her words. "But I've never seen him like
this. The palace staff are afraid to look him in the eye, some
won't even enter the same room. Even Arif finds Zafir hard
to handle nowadays, I hear."

Lauren felt a perverse satisfaction at the thought of upsetting Zafir's old mentor. It was Arif who had discovered the truth of her pregnancy. With hindsight, she resented him less for telling the truth and more for knowing her private affairs. "Good. Everyone is learning what a jerk your sheikh is."

She thought Farrah would explode at her, instead, a grin split her mouth, and relief shuddered through Lauren. Farrah had come to mean so much to her already and not because she was the only one who spoke her mind. "You should talk to him, get to know him. It might relieve the tension between you two, and the staff, too."

"How?" The word rang around them with all her frustration packed into it. "How will I ask him anything if he doesn't even see me? For all his proclamations about wanting the best for the baby, he hasn't inquired once."

"I report to him every night, with orders to contact him immediately if you even feel a twinge of discomfort."

Okay, so he was keeping tabs on her. "Can you help me convince the guards to escort me to his suite?"

Even before she completed the sentence, Farrah shook her head. "That's forbidden and…scandalous."

"Because there's no scandal surrounding me already?" she said, unable to staunch the bitterness that crept into her words. "Because all of Behraat hasn't already decided that I'm the sheikh's Western plaything?"

Except he hadn't *played* with her, despite the threats he had made. God, how much more twisted and perverse could she get about him?

The tightening of Farrah's mouth was enough to confirm Lauren's suspicions. "No one who has seen Zafir with you would assume anything, but…" Sighing, Farrah looked at her. "The Zafir I know would never take away a woman's freedom. If you'd known Tariq, you would see how different Zafir is, especially, when it comes to women."

But only she'd hidden an important truth from him.

Lauren slid down into the velvet recliner. Little niggles of doubt shaking her will lose.

Had she fallen into the very trap she had been intent on avoiding? Put herself first and not her child? Had she reacted only out of hurt and jealousy?

Had Zafir been right, after all?

Burying her head in her hands, she groaned. It had been wrong to take away his right to know.

She had to apologize, make him understand she had never meant to cut him out of the child's life. She had to swallow her insecurities, move past her vulnerability when it came to him.

And accept that Zafir wanted to be a part of her child's life. Much as she wished she never had to lay eyes on him ever again.

That evening, Lauren felt refreshed after a brisk walk in the lush private gardens, sealed off from the outer world by an eight-foot red brick wall.

Two guards always flanked her, even over the little distance she went. And she didn't believe it was for protection as Farrah had tried to convince her, as if Lauren was of value to anyone.

More like surveillance, because His Royal Highness didn't trust her.

She entered the sitting area and stilled.

Zafir was lounging on the velvet-lined couch, his head tilted back and his eyes closed.

She pulled the tall twin doors that weighed a ton with a vicious tug, intending to slam them but holding on to her frustration took more than she had.

Her heart beating noticeably faster at his mere presence, she studied him greedily. The setting sun behind him cast an orange glow that lovingly caressed the angles and planes of his face. His long legs sprawled out carelessly in front of him drawing her attention to the sinewy strength of his thighs. A white dress shirt, with gold cuff links and unbuttoned halfway emphasized that raw masculinity of his arms. The leanly muscled expanse of bronzed chest underneath sent tingles to places she'd rather not think about in his presence.

The more she saw Zafir in his natural element, the more she couldn't believe that he'd been attracted to her in the first place.

She wasn't plain-looking, she admitted that much. But he…he was magnificently masculine, starkly sensual, like the harshly beautiful elements of the very desert had come together to mold him. Even in that dormant state, a pulse of energy radiated from him.

"Are you quite done with your perusal, *habeebti*?"

Husky, low, his voice touched her skin like a charge of electricity. To occupy her hands, she unwound the silk scarf she had wrapped around her neck.

"I've been rendered mute that you remember my existence."

Her hands not quite steady, she poured herself a glass of water.

The water slid down her throat coolly. She pressed the glass to her face and groaned, hoping he would put down the heat in her cheeks to the weather.

His gaze flew open and traveled over her with a thorough possessiveness that wound her up even tighter. Hands clasped behind his head, the action pulling his shirt tighter across his chest, the dark shadow of his skin was a visual feast.

"Farrah was right, you did miss me. If I had known you were so *hungry* for the sight of me, I would have come sooner."

Her mouth fell open and she just stared, unable to even mumble a token retort. Even seething with the knowledge that he was turning her life upside down, she was starved for the sight of him.

She walked around the couch to the opposite side, needing the distance between them. Extremely conscious, she tugged the flimsy edge of her sheer yellow cotton blouse.

Which was absolutely the wrong thing to do, because his smoldering gaze moved slowly over her mouth to her throat and her chest.

He tilted forward suddenly with a contained violence. She jerked back instantly and the back of her knees hit the couch. "What are you walking around in?"

She remained resolutely mute.

"No snarky response?" he goaded, and she had a feeling he was looking for a fight. Or something else, a voice whispered, stretching her nerves unbearably tight. For all his smooth tone, there was an edge of something darker at play.

"I…was too hot," she replied softly, striving to rid her voice of that mutinous tone. "The guards, they barely look at me, much as they're equally fascinated and disgusted by what I represent within these palace walls."

He leveled a look of pure disbelief at her. But she would behave like an adult if it killed her, she decided. "All of Behraat is fascinated with you right now, and plotting about how best to use you to damage me."

"Am I in danger then?"

Hard and unrelenting, his gaze held hers. "Yes. But the only kind that would actually get to you is from me."

"Even my love for this baby won't make it tolerable to be confined to these palace walls for the rest of my life, Zafir. I need—"

"I don't have any other role for you." *Which is why I walked out*, his unsaid explanation fluttered in the silence between them.

There it was, the answer to the question that had plagued her since he had locked her up.

"I'm not asking for one." Throat thick with something she couldn't even name, she looked at her hands. "I wasn't supposed to be in Behraat, I wasn't supposed to know your real identity and I definitely wasn't supposed to get pregnant, was I?"

"No, you were not." The statement was matter-of-fact, no bitterness, no regret, no blame. She wished she had his flair for that acceptance.

"I had control over this attraction when you devoured me with those big eyes on that night in the ER. Or that minute the next morning when I kissed you at the end of your shift. Or the next night when I returned to your apartment after I dropped off Huma and you opened the door and invited me in. Or when I, even knowing what awaited me, came back to you again and again. Not now."

"Easy for you to accept it, because nothing changes in your life."

"Believe that if it helps you hate me." His head fell back against the couch, and his eyes closed again. "Don't drive that fruit knife into me while I rest. It will plunge Behraat into chaos."

"I'll control my murderous urges for now," she quipped, noting the blue shadows under his eyes, the gaunt look to his features.

He was king of the palace and he wanted to rest here?

Sighing, she uncoiled her legs to move away from him.

Instantly, his hand shot out and clasped her wrist. Streaks of heat from his thumb on her veins. "No, stay.

"I like having you next to me, your heart beating rapidly, your nerves stretched to the hilt, your head saying no and your body saying yes, while you wonder whether I will touch you or not, kiss you or not. Whether this will be the day when you surrender your will to me.

"It relaxes me, unlike the myriad delights the palace offers."

A gasp escaped her, half outraged, half laughing. "You're a sadist."

"Hmm."

She settled back against the chaise, her hand trapped still in his.

"Maybe keeping a *helpless, pregnant woman captive*—" A bark of disbelieving laughter escaped him and it was a dart shot straight to her heart "—is haunting you at night and you can't sleep?" Her hand reached out to push a lock of hair from his forehead.

Only when she saw her pale fingers against the backdrop of that high forehead did she realize what she was doing. Snatching it back, she fisted it in her lap. "You look awful." And because she couldn't bear for him to think she was concerned, she added, "Is the world not bowing and scraping enough to Your Highness?"

Uncomfortable silence lingered as he slowly opened his eyes. Studied her. She saw him hesitate and then sigh. A wealth of emotion reverberated in that soft exhale. "It's more likely due to a couple of nights spent by my comatose father's bed because the doctors think he might have moved a finger."

Lauren finally identified the emotion radiating from him.

Grief.

He was grieving and he'd come to her. Somehow, Lauren couldn't stop thinking they were connected, couldn't stop her mind from jumping to a thousand different conclusions. Curiosity trampled her every effort to keep him at a distance, shattered the safety net of her hatred.

"Every couple of weeks, I'm told that consciousness is within his grasp. So I wait by his bedside to tell him that my brother, his firstborn, is dead, so that I can push him that last step to his death, and put both of us out of our misery."

The pain in his voice gutted Lauren, the resignation in it so unlike the man she knew.

"I'm the man who ordered the death of his brother so that he can rule Behraat."

Those words slammed into her. How easily she had buried her head in her own fears and insecurities, how egotistic to believe that she was the center of his world?

His father was in a coma, his brother recently dead...to take up the rule of Behraat in such a volatile climate, she couldn't imagine what he was going through.

"I'm sorry for your loss."

"Hmm?" he said absentmindedly, his gaze lingering on her neck. She fought to sit still under the scrutiny.

"If his chopper hadn't been caught in that desert sandstorm and led to his death, Tariq would have been captured and...executed. Under my order.

"If he were here, I would pick up a gun and shoot him again for what he did to Behraat, for what he did to..." He flexed his fingers as though he could feel the gun in his hand. "Do you still feel sorry for me?"

Guilt and grief reverberated in each word he spoke. She held on to his gaze steadily while her insides quivered. He didn't want her sympathy, in fact, his words were tinged with warning.

She ran a hand over her tummy, more to distract him than to calm herself. "I'm actually wondering how I'd explain all this family history to the baby without sounding like we're a couple of nutcases, y'know? Murdering father, untrustworthy mother..."

A light came on in those golden eyes, chasing away the shadows. His grin tugged at her. "We have annihilated any chance of normality the poor child had, yes?"

She laughed, the tightness in her chest loosening. They could hate each other all they wanted, but they shared a bond through this child. And it filled her with immense joy and sadness. "Definitely. But then normal is overrated, don't you think?"

She loved it when she could laugh with him like this, when she could bring that warm light to his eyes.

"Is there anything I can do to help, Zafir?"

That gaze, amused and fiery, jerked to hers and she instantly wanted to snatch her words back. He turned his neck this way and that. "Work those magical fingers over my neck."

The last time she had touched him for that so-called massage... *Casablanca* had been forgotten, their pizza had gotten cold...

The same knowledge glittered in his languorous gaze, stoked over her, a whisper of sinful promises and sensual delights. She ran a hand over her neck, feeling wound up pretty tight.

"Find yourself a damn masseuse, Zafir. Isn't Behraat crawling with women ready to serve His Royal Highness?"

He grinned. His uncut hair falling over his forehead, he looked like a carefree rogue. But he wasn't. The more she learned of him, the more she realized that New York had been a taste of the forbidden for both her and him.

"I did have two proposals of marriage this past week from the fathers of two beautiful, young, traditional Behraati girls. Every man's dream."

And just like that, any goodwill she had cultivated vanished, the very thought of Zafir with his bride scouring her in a place she desperately wanted to erase.

She leveled a breezy smile at him while she felt brittle inside. "They sound perfect for you, Zafir.

"Women ready to do your bidding without a word of protest, ready to please you in bed when you want to get laid, willing to fade into the background when you forget their existence," she said bitchily, offering up a silent apology to the women in question, "why not take one of them up on their offer and let me be?"

He was next to her in two seconds, his rock-hard thigh wedged sinfully against hers.

She strove to hold herself still, but with his hand behind her, she had nowhere to go on the couch.

He pushed a lock of hair from her forehead, the simple touch evoking a fierce need within her. His breath caressed her lips, the scent of him, rich musk breathing under exotic sandalwood, drugged the very air she breathed.

"It would make life easy for me. But I don't want any of them." His hands kneaded the stiff muscles in her shoulders turning them into liquid mush. "I want you, the one I shouldn't want. The High Council fears it right, I think."

"What do they fear?"

"That somehow you have bewitched me."

She closed her eyes to shut out the image of him, digging deep within herself to find the strength to fight. There was none.

Only memories lingered, memories that shifted and shaped themselves into coherence now. As though she needed to look through this lens to understand the full significance of her relationship with Zafir.

She caught his hand with hers, intending to push him away, instead, he linked his fingers with hers, the little hairs on his forearm rubbing against hers.

Her gaze drifted downward to the bulge in his trousers and she was on instant, incinerating fire. "You ignored me for three weeks. You're stressed again now and you want sex. Just like in New York." There it was, the common denominator. "So you decided to pay me a visit. Like I was a hooker who knows your special needs. Like you were a junkie and I your fix."

A growl fell from his mouth. "You're determined to cheapen yourself, aren't you?"

She shrugged. "Calling it like I see it."

Gripping her arms, he forced her to look at him. "Yes, every time, I received news about another atrocity committed by Tariq, every time I felt rage run feral in my veins, every time I thought I would die a little more inside if I didn't seize Behraat from him, every time I thought I wouldn't see my father again... I came to you...

"I came to you and I lost myself in you until my sanity was back, until I had control over myself again, until that powerless rage cleared.

"But it was not cheap."

Hoarse and powerful, his words demolished her fragile defenses in one fell swoop. "Zafir," she protested, sinking sinuously deep into his spell.

One long finger traced the seam of her lower lip, pressed it, sending fresh shivers spewing into her skin. He lifted her toward him until she sat astride him. The soft silk of his trousers or her cotton leggings were no barrier to the hard length of his arousal fitting so perfectly against her core.

She was like putty in his arms, her will nonexistent.

A whimper wrenched from her and he caught it with his mouth, his lean frame shuddering around her.

If he had used that honed body to seduce her, if he had used those skillful hands to wrench her response, she would have resisted him, somehow. But instead, his gaze blazing with such depth of hunger, he pulled her down to meet his mouth.

Jagged and desperate, his words were a lash against her senses. "Do not deny us this, Lauren..."

It was the closest he'd ever come to saying please and the most *she would ever amount* to in his life.

She turned away at the last second, need and agony twisted together into a rope that bound her to him.

He dragged his mouth against her throat, open and

searing, infusing her skin with delirious need, whispering words she couldn't understand. Sharp, spiraling pleasure forked through her lower belly.

Ripped of even a semblance of sanity or control, she moved up over him in an age-old instinct, rubbing the crease of her aching core against his hardness. One large hand stayed on her hip, kneading possessively while the other cupped her breast.

Wet heat from his roving mouth branded the skin at her neck, her nipple tightening boldly against his palm.

Shivering and shaking, she sank her fingers into his hair, draped herself over him like a clinging vine.

"Too long, I've needed this for too long, *habeebti…*"

Then he was whispering words of reverent praise into the valley of her breasts, his hands running over her arms in soothing strokes as if she was a filly he had to calm and then he was sinking his hands under her blouse, and his big, rough palm came to rest on her not-so-flat-anymore midriff…

And the world froze. Their gazes collided while their breaths huffed noisily around them.

Heavy and abrasive, the weight of his palm scorched her. "Your body is…" he sounded stunned as his gaze ate her up "…different already?"

Lauren jerked back so hard that she fell out of his lap, onto the floor. The edge of the coffee table hit the back of her head and she gasped as pain thudded through the back of her head and to the front.

And then she was scrambling away from him, so afraid that he would catch her, so afraid that she had no defense left. So afraid that he would want no more from her than sex, that he would never give more of himself to her, that one day, he would be done with her and walk away.

And to wonder why he had, it would become the vicious cycle of her life.

But there had been such longing in his gaze when he had gentled his hand on her abdomen, such a deep hunger in that unguarded moment.

It was like handing her a grenade in the middle of a war.

If she had to admit defeat, if she had to give in, she would make sure he paid a price, too.

Yes, something inside her roared.

Make him pay for your surrender.

His obsession with her was becoming dangerous, Zafir realized as he panted hard. The scent of her swirled around him like a net, ensnaring his senses, obliterating rationality.

Swollen and pink, her mouth was tempting enough to give his soul over. Her breasts fell and rose fast, her lithe body bristling with emotion.

She looked like a wild deer, cornered but defiant.

All he'd wanted was to bury himself in her willing body, escape the relentless fury, the powerless grief that continued to ravage him as he sat by his father.

All he'd wanted while the politics and power plays continued around him was her. Only this sensuous creature that pierced the loneliness, the only one who had seen the real him. And wanted him.

"Come back here, Lauren," he said smoothly. "I want to confirm you're not hurt," he said, gritting his jaw when she stepped back again.

Something chased across her angular face. Not need, not fear, but challenge.

He felt like the wild thing in her eyes had electrocuted him.

"You don't have to chase me, Your Highness," she said while she grabbed the small opening of her blouse with both hands. The rip of the thin cotton was like a tribal drum in the silence. "I surrender," she said so softly and yet in a voice that carved through him.

The edges of her blouse fell away, exposing the curves of her plump breasts cupped in white silk, the dainty dip of her waist, flaring into hips he had anchored himself on so many times. The shadow of her dark nipples was barely hidden by the silk. Color streaked her cheeks, and her neck.

Slowly, he brought his gaze to her face, something in her stance dousing cold water on his need.

"You win," she declared, and his ire rose slowly.

He didn't want her like this, like spoils of a war he'd won. "What the hell are you talking about?" he said cornering her.

But this time, she didn't step back. Stubborn chin held high, she stood her ground.

She pushed the blouse off her shoulders and reached for the hem of her skirt. "Should I shower and ready myself for you or do you need instant gratification? You want to have me here or on the bed?"

The breath knocked out of him as if someone had jammed a fist in his throat.

"Enough, Lauren."

"No. This is what you are turning me into. Tucked away in this palace, cut off from the world, waiting on tenterhooks, wondering if you'll see me again...wondering what my child's place is going to be in your world..."

"I would love her or him more than anything in the world." He heard the words after he spoke them, realizing the truth.

Something flashed in her gaze before she drove it away. "But you will treat his mother as if she were disposable?

"It was wrong to hide the truth from you, I admit it.

"But you...you decided, from the beginning, that this is all I'm good for. So let's do it the proper way."

She moved toward the chaise longue and pushed away the myriad of colorful pillows from it. "Do you want me to face you or the other way around? Or would you prefer me on my knees?"

He flinched. "Cover yourself."

When she stood like that brazenly, he picked up a velvet throw.

She trembled at his touch, so stiff and tensed like a stretched bow, teetering on the edge, and yet determined to fight this. Determined to fight him and herself.

Dirty, was that what this was? Was that what he had made of them?

In that moment, he fought that loneliness, that craving for her body, that yearning to lose himself in her arms, this struggle his father must have fought with himself and lost, turning his mother into a whore in the eyes of her family, her tribe and the world, turning Zafir into an orphan.

And Zafir won.

He would never become a slave to his body's needs. He would not ruin Lauren's life, the mother of his child's life, simply because he wanted something he couldn't have.

Without another glance at her, he walked away.

CHAPTER SEVEN

Bear with the prison until the baby is here, until I can ensure your safety. We will discuss it again. I will not give up on my child, however.
—Zafir

LAUREN STARED AT the careless scrawl on the softest paper printed with the seal of the Al Masood house for the thousandth time. Farrah's voice across the sitting room sounded far away as she pushed out a shaky breath.

Only one thought lingered since she'd seen him a week ago.

If she had saved herself from a fate she loathed—becoming his mistress—why did it feel as if she had lost him all over again?

At least, he was willing to reevaluate, the first sign of which had been when she'd been informed that she could visit the famous open bazaar that she'd been dying to go to since day one.

She'd stupidly assumed Zafir was coming.

Foolish Lauren.

Instead, armed with a maid and three guards, she'd set off, eager to be out of the palace.

It had been dusty, crowded, hot and a glorious sensory whir of spices and sounds, unlike anything she had ever seen.

Colorful, sprawling tents and shops set up on both sides of a long, winding street sold handwoven scarves, authentic handicrafts, antique hookahs, thick syrupy dates that Lauren had washed down with cold mint sherbet, set against the backdrop of the redbrick buildings that were centuries old.

Every step she took, she wished Zafir was there, showing her the sights, mocking her when she refused to try a new dish.

Laughing, she had haggled for five minutes over an intricately designed antique silver bracelet, aware that she was being fleeced as a foreigner.

Until the youngest and the nicest of her guards, Ahmed, had chivalrously interfered and it became obvious to the street vendor and the crowd around her that she wasn't just any tourist.

The sudden silence that had emerged amid the ruckus had been so unnerving.

She was the sheikh's mistress, an instant spectacle drawing curiosity, disgust and even pity in some generous eyes. In the blink of an eye, she'd understood why Zafir confined her to the palace.

Noticing Farrah's worried face, Lauren got up from the recliner. "What's going on?"

"There are two women going into labor right now. One family is high powered and I'll have to attend her at her house. The other one's in a village that borders the city. The other ob-gyn is out of town and her husband won't let her see male doctors."

She pulled her phone from her handbag and made another call.

"Any luck?" Lauren asked.

Farrah shook her head.

It was as simple as her next breath for Lauren. "I'll attend the other one."

Farrah's gaze flew to Lauren, relief dancing in it. Until she was shaking her head again. "Zafir would never allow it. And I can't even ask because he left this morning to visit the States. I—"

"That's absurd. We're talking about a woman who needs medical attention. Are you going to let your fear of Zafir dictate her fate? I'll take Ahmed with me and hopefully will be back tomorrow morning at the worst. Come on, Farrah. I'll lose my mind sitting here, knowing I could help."

Farrah studied her for several heart-stopping seconds. "Have you delivered before?"

"Yes."

"Fine," Farrah said with a sigh. "But please, please be careful, yes? She's had a smooth pregnancy so far, so there shouldn't be any complications." She tugged Lauren's hands into hers. "Lauren, this woman, the tribe to which she belongs to, they don't…consider themselves part of Behraat, her husband—he's been defying their rules to bring her to the clinic—"

"Doesn't mean they don't deserve medical attention."

"No, it doesn't." Farrah smiled. "Just be careful. Zafir will skin me alive if anything happens to you." But it was clear that her mind was already on the task in hand. "The moment I'm free, I'll be at the clinic."

Adrenaline spurring her into action, Lauren nodded. For the first time in so many weeks, she felt a sense of purpose.

While Farrah made another call, Lauren crammed energy bars and bottles of water, and a loose cardigan into her backpack. Then she changed into a freshly laundered white kaftan and loose cotton trousers, also in white, as it was the best fabric for the heat. She braided her hair tightly and wrapped a silk scarf loosely around her hair and neck. Catching Farrah's curious gaze, she stilled. "I don't want to draw attention to myself." She patted her hand over her not-so-flat tummy. "Do I look—?"

"Yes." Farrah answered without hesitation. "But pregnant or not, American or not, you're not average. No wonder Zafir lost his head over you."

Something in her tone tugged at Lauren.

Within minutes, they were walking out of Zafir's private quarters, through the marble-tiled corridors. A state-of-the-art elevator brought them to the underground parking lot where a man in uniform was waiting next to a rugged jeep that she only saw in *Survivor*-type shows.

Checking to see that the medical file Farrah had emailed downloaded onto her phone, she climbed into the jeep.

"No wonder he lost his head over you." She clutched Farrah's words to her heart foolishly and waited for the envoy to leave.

Zafir closed the door to his office, bone-tired after his four-day trip to the United States to discuss a new treaty regarding Behraat's oil supply to the Western nation.

His first official trip abroad and all he had heard was: stability in their region of the world, and Behraat's particular lack of it in the past three years. About all the feathers Tariq had ruffled since his father's coma.

For a blistering cowardly moment, Zafir had indulged in not returning. And just as soon discarded the fanciful notion.

He needed to pick a side in the divisive High Council, needed to pick one of their daughters they paraded like horses under his nose for his bride and be done with it.

Behraat needed it. He as the High Sheikh needed to show stability, his commitment as a ruler to both his people and the outside world.

But all he thought of was Lauren, her soft mouth and her mewling moans and her trembling body. The tears on her proud face, the regret in her expression when she had admitted that she'd been wrong...

The door to his office burst open. He bit back the scathing words that rose to his lips at the sight of Farrah, fear etched into her unlined face. Followed closely by a stone-faced Arif.

Unknown dread fisted his throat.

"Zafir," Farrah said, "Lauren…she has been kidnapped."

His chest felt as if there was a vise clamping it. "She… *what*?" he mumbled, his voice barely recognizable to his own ears. "How?"

"*She*," Arif still wouldn't utter Lauren's name, "convinced Farrah to let her help the Dahab tribe woman who went into labor just as Farrah was getting ready to attend another woman."

The mere mention of the Dahab made his heart thud.

"And?" he exploded.

"By the time I got there…" Farrah was distraught. "No one knew where Lauren was. The Dahab woman, her baby, her husband, even Ahmed, were all gone."

"When was this?"

"Three days ago."

With a growl, Zafir pushed at his chair.

The revolving chair crashed into the chest behind him, scattering the contents—a flower vase, and a framed photo of his father that fell to the rug with a soft thump.

Lauren's face swam into his vision, fear stealing his very thoughts. If something happened to her all because he had selfishly involved her in his life…

He ran a hand over his forehead, the headache that had been coming on all day crystallizing into a pounding behind his eyes.

Farrah stepped toward him, her hands clasped together in front of her. "I'm so sorry, Zafir."

But knowing Lauren's stubborn will, he couldn't blame Farrah.

"I sent a message to the Dahab in your name," Arif said, "but as usual, they have ignored any communication. The palace guard reports them traveling east into the desert."

Had they taken her because she was carrying his child? As revenge against his father?

Dahab didn't care for the ways of the outside world including Behraat.

But they had good reason to hate his family. If his father had brought shame on them, Tariq had hunted them across the desert. Every instinct clamored to order his Special Forces Air Team, to use his might to pluck Lauren from their midst.

But he couldn't.

Even if it was a huge risk to Lauren and his unborn child, he had to do it the peaceful way.

"Arrange transportation for me, alone." If he descended on them with men and weapons, the rift would only widen and become something he couldn't resolve in his lifetime. "If they harm her in any way, they'll face my wrath," he said, knowing that he would destroy everything in his path if she even had a scratch.

Lauren shot up from the worn-out divan, a sound hurling her from the hazy edges of her afternoon nap into wide-eyed alertness in the space of a breath.

The chief of the tribe had ensured her that she'd be safe with them, that no one would harm her, when they'd asked her to accompany them three days ago. But the pitch-black of the night outside the tent, the thick silence that descended when the encampment settled for the night, had unnerved Lauren.

Yet she'd learned she'd been right to trust him. Even though he had accompanied her, she hadn't seen Ahmed once they had reached the Dahab's encampment though. Nor had there had been any word from Farrah, which worried her the most.

Then she realized what had woken her up. She saw the

long shadow, clearly male, over the silk partition that curtained the room off from the rest of the tent.

She was rubbing her eyes when Zafir marched inside, his broad frame shrinking the tent. Greedy for the sight of him, she drank him in.

There were dark shadows under his eyes. His jet-black hair was rumpled in a sexy, inviting, run-your-fingers-through-me way, as if he had already done that numerous times. His white cotton shirt and light blue jeans did nothing to dampen the effect of his masculinity.

She'd barely drawn a breath when she was ensconced against a hard chest. Hands anchored on his hips, she shuddered. Rough hands moved over her back urgently, the upper curve of her bottom, her hips, her stomach...and stilled. Heart slamming hard against her rib cage, Lauren held herself still while the scent of desert and pure, intoxicating male filled her nostrils.

A soundless whimper ricocheted through her as her body adjusted against his hard muscles.

Soft pressure on her nape tilted her head up. A scowl pulled his brows together, his eyes shimmering golden with emotion she'd never glimpsed before.

Mouth groggy, belly knotted, she squeaked out his name. "Zafir?"

Seconds passed before he responded but it felt like an eternity. Tenderness flew from his fingers where he clasped her cheeks. "You look tired."

Her throat hoarse, she nodded, sinking into his embrace foolishly.

Just one minute, she told herself. Just one minute before she reminded herself why this wasn't a good idea.

But that minute was barely done before she was released.

Blinking, she looked up at him.

Hard edges, inscrutable expression, thinned mouth, everything she didn't like about him was back.

"Pack your things. We're leaving," he said dismissively, his gaze taking in her tent.

Stuffing her few things into her backpack, Lauren turned and found the tent ominously empty.

Ahmed stood outside, a paleness under his tanned skin, his gaze dutifully shied away from her.

Zafir, his gaze not leaving her, listened with his head bowed to the chief of the tribe. Lauren nodded and smiled when the new mom Salma pressed a silk scarf into her hands and hugged her.

A small crowd of women and children waved at her while men surrounded Zafir and the chief, but at a distance. But Lauren could feel the distrust and animosity that surrounded him.

Had she caused trouble for him again?

Coffee-colored dunes stretched toward the horizon in front of her while the Dahab encampments lay behind her. The same 4x4 was idling on the road.

When Ahmed, without touching her, nodded for her to move toward the vehicle, she searched for Zafir.

His thundering presence beside her robbed her words. "Do me the small courtesy of pretending I can control you, yes?" he gritted through his teeth. A low vibration raced along her lower back.

Instantly, his hold loosened. Swallowing her flippant "thank you" for his condescending tone, she nodded.

Within minutes, Zafir and she hurtled along the rough track, hugging narrow paths through the dunes.

"Aren't we returning to the city?" she asked and got a sharp "no" in answer.

Pulling her gaze away from that chiseled profile, she kept her hands in her lap.

Zafir's mind raced like the sand that flew from dune to dune shifting the very landscape of the harsh desert.

His anxiety about Lauren had lasted two minutes after he had entered the chief's tent.

Shame had his fingers tighten over the steering wheel as he remembered the chief's disbelief at Zarif's accusations.

"Your father and you have forgotten tradition, our roots, the very fabric that makes the Bedouin life."

Every word, spoken in a soft yet steely tone, was true.

To assume that they would have harmed a hair on Lauren, on any woman, pregnant or otherwise, had been pure ignorance and blind prejudice.

The tribes were known for their hospitality, their generosity to even an enemy requesting shelter, legendary.

"We give our women protection, a respectable place in life. Not keep them as prisoners or mistresses."

That statement lashed against his sense of honor.

Knowing the route to the oasis like the back of his hand, he chanced a glance at Lauren. Her head tilted back against the seat, and her eyes closed, he saw the resolute tilt of her chin, the long line of her throat, her fingers laced tightly in her lap.

Still, there was a knot in his chest, a leftover from his fear for her and the baby.

"This woman carrying your child is brave, kind, strong…" the chief had said. *"Marry her, Zafir. Make her your sheikha and we will end this enmity between the tribes and the state. We will forget what your father did to one of our daughters."*

Bringing the tribes back into the fold would be the advantage he needed. Not even the High Council could fault his power, or his reign then. For he would be fixing a fracture in the very fabric of their nation.

Behraat would be strong and one again, after three decades of being torn apart by his father's selfish and scandalous pursuit of a young, innocent woman from the tribes.

All he had to do was marry the woman carrying his

child, the woman that set fire to his blood, the woman who…

Might hate to be used as a pawn in his game for power, his conscience piped up.

It is a gift, Zafir, some devil inside his head said. *It's the one gift you have received in your hard, betrayed, duty-bound, cursed life,* it whispered.

Lauren and this child and the ability to finally unite Behraat and rule it, it was all a gift.

She had always wanted his commitment, a definition to their relationship, hadn't she?

Here it was. The biggest commitment he had ever made, except to Behraat.

He couldn't squander this gift.

Not if it would bring legitimacy to his child and his power.

CHAPTER EIGHT

THEY TRAVELED ON for what seemed like the better part of an hour. Lauren fidgeted in her seat, trying to work out a kink in her shoulder.

"Are you uncomfortable?" Came the instant question from Zafir.

"I'm fine."

The track vanished halfway through, until it seemed as if they climbed hundreds of feet up a giant ocher sand mound that offered panoramic views of the desert floor and then suddenly evened out again.

Her eyes wide, Lauren took in the landscape as the jeep came to a halt.

Miles and miles of rippled, undulating dunes rose in all four directions, the harsh beauty of it stealing her breath. Against the backdrop of the desolate sands lay a lush encampment, eons away in scale and quality from the Dahab's tents, a stark contrast to the stretching emptiness.

Tall palms behind the two curved tents formed a dense circular perimeter as far as she could see. The early evening sun streaked everything reddish orange.

It was breathtaking, tremendous, and it made her concerns seem so small.

She pulled out her cell phone. But remembered her battery had drained a few hours after she had arrived at the Dahab camp.

Hearing Zafir's tread, she turned around. "Do you have your phone?"

He looked at her outstretched hand, beating a path up

her arm, her neck and then settling on her face. Something shimmered in his eyes then. A possessive glint. A triumphant light that sent goose bumps over her skin even under the relentless heat. "It's a little late to call for help." But he pulled his phone out.

Grabbing the phone from his hand, she turned around to click a selfie with the dazzling encampment behind her. She knew she was acting a little juvenile and a lot irreverent tourist but after that glimpse of fire in his eyes and the absence of another soul around for as far as she could see, she wasn't eager to go into the tent.

"Is there no one else here?"

Something gleamed in his eyes. "The servants are trained to be not seen or heard."

Which didn't help her any. "Could you take a pic for me?"

"*A pic?*" he repeated with quiet murder in his tone.

"Yes." She placed her hands on her hips. "And no, I won't sell pictures of the Sheikh of Behraat's oasis hideaway in the desert even if I was paid a million dollars." She swiped a trickle of sweat from her forehead. "As far as I can see, there's no interrogation room here either, so come on."

With a sudden movement that made her heart crawl to her throat, he grabbed the phone from her hand, and marched to the entrance and held the flap open.

Do not poke the grumpy bear, Lauren.

She entered the tent.

A burst of rich color, deep purples and sheer violets, greeted her everywhere she looked. Brass tables set with more lanterns and tea lights, handcrafted rugs strewed around, it was a sight to behold. Two veiled areas separated away from the lounge where they stood.

One had a myriad of dishes laid out on low tables guessing by the delicious aroma wafting toward her and the other contained a low but vast bed with a million pillows of all shapes and sizes on it. Bed big enough for two. A thick fur rug lay neatly folded at the bottom while a small brass-legged washstand with a basin stood against the far corner.

Swallowing the sudden tension, she faced the silent six-foot-two-inch male staring at her. His very silence sent her nerves thrumming. "I like it. Which tent is yours?" she said with a cheer that hurt her own head.

"This."

Thud went her heart against her rib cage. "The other one's mine then?"

She moved to his side, or tried to. Viselike fingers clamped her arm and pulled her to the seating area behind them.

With precise movements that actually betrayed his ruffled temper, he poured water into a copper tumbler and handed it to her. "Drink before you expire from the heat."

She took the tumbler and drank the water without a word. Choosing the divan farthest from him, she sank onto it. The bed was soft and comfy so she tucked her legs beneath her and leaned against the tent wall.

Heart tattooing in her chest, she lifted her head and met his gaze. Before he could take the little place left next to her, she groaned and stretched her legs, tilting to the side.

Something like a curse fell from his mouth before he chose the divan perpendicular to hers. His long legs spread out before him, he sat straight unlike her. As if he suspected that she would run and he would need to pounce.

"Where do you think I'm going to run to," she said slowly.

His head jerked up, his entire frame unnaturally still. "You're the most infuriating, exhausting woman I've ever met."

Fury. Impatience. Worry. She frowned at the last.

"Are you hungry?"

She shook her head while casting her mind around to find any excuse to postpone the storm she could sense brewing between them. There was a sense of calculation, a sense of coiled energy about him, as if he was deciding what to do with her and it let loose panic in her tummy.

Looking down at her wrinkled tunic, she scrunched her nose. "I need a shower and an early night. I didn't get my turn to shower this evening before you stormed in there." She added a little sigh to that to convince him.

His eyes narrowed.

"I spent most of the last two nights by Salma's side helping her while she recuperated."

The muscles in his face relaxed, just enough to let her breathe fully. "Why you? Where were her mother and aunts?"

"Bashir's continual presence in the tent chased them off."

"Bashir?"

"Her husband. Salma lost a lot of blood and he's determined to help her with the night feedings, and changing the baby and burping her and so on… Apparently, the women in the camp thinks it's scandalous for him to be spending so much time with her when she's not up to her usual duties yet."

This time, he frowned. And she thought how cute he looked when he didn't understand something. Which was very rare. "What usual duties?"

"Really, Zafir… *Her wifely duties*," she said with an arch to her tone.

Understanding dawned in his golden gaze. He ran a hand through his hair and she wondered if he was trying not to look at her. He cleared his throat then, and Lauren knew, just knew, that he didn't want to hear any more.

So, of course, she elaborated.

"They seemed to think Bashir wanting to help his wife

when he couldn't get sex out of her was strange and shocking. Imagine that.

"Even Salma was shy at first but I convinced her that it was very important for the baby to bond with the father as well as the mother, for them as a family."

His gaze jerked to hers and held it. Challenge simmered there and her gut swooped. "What was she shy about?"

She shrugged, cursing herself inwardly for the heat rising up her neck. "I told Salma that feeding the baby in front of her husband is the most natural thing in the world and that she should be glad that she has a husband who wanted to pitch in and do the dirty work, not just strut around like a peacock and announce that his boys were good swimmers."

His long fingers pressed at his temple and then rubbed his face. But he couldn't quite hide the amusement in his eyes. "You did not say that."

"I did." The expression she'd seen on the couple's faces made her grin. "Bashir dropped a pile of baby clothes while Salma, with a blank face, said they didn't have boys. He wouldn't meet my gaze for the rest of the night. Once he left, she asked me to explain.

"When I did, she was both amazed and a little horrified, I think."

"Not all men strut around claiming that their…" A dark flush claimed his cheeks. "Whatever it is you said. I didn't strut."

"Well, you're not really the strutting kind."

"No?" His mouth twitched now. "I feel as though my machismo has been reduced. What kind am I?"

"Please. Like you don't know."

It was his turn to shrug now. "I would like to hear it in your words."

"Blatant sexuality oozes out of every pore in your body, Zafir." Warmth pooled below her skin at her own words.

"Six years of sexual drought and it took you three days. You made me feel as if I was the most attractive woman in the world. As if I was the only one to have shredded that tight control of yours. Hell of a trick that," she said, aware of how powerless her attraction to him always left her.

"It was not a trick. Whatever you felt, multiply it by ten times and you'll understand how I felt."

The divan shifted as Zafir's weight sank into it and every cell in her froze.

Golden eyes stared back at her. His elbows on his legs, he was leaning forward.

"So are you going to want help with night feedings and such when the baby comes? Is there a class we should be attending together to learn about these things?"

It was the cruelest thing he could have asked her. Like a mirage in the desert that could tempt and warp one's sense of reality. That promised to quench your unbearable thirst when there was not a drop.

He had no right to ask such things of her when they were anything but a married couple absolutely in love with each other.

Donning a smile that threatened to crack her face with its brittleness, she went for playfulness. No way would she ever betray how dismayed she felt. "There's going to be an army of maids and nannies at my command, right?" Her neck hurt at how stiffly she held herself.

She took his silence as a yes.

"Then you'll be excused. I'm sure you'll be super busy with state affairs to…" She shrugged the rest of her answer away.

The tent reverberated with something unsaid, yet Lauren didn't know what. Unless it was her brittle smile cracking into pieces.

Zafir stood to leave. Pausing at the entrance to the tent,

he looked back at her. "I will send a maid. You can wash in the oasis and rest. Is there anything you need?"

The moment she shook her head, he was gone.

Zafir heard the splash around the oasis while he walked the perimeter, like he had done since Rashid had brought him here a long time ago.

Once he had discovered his father's duplicity, he had not come here again. Loathed to mar this place with bitter reality, he realized now.

He had always felt great pride when he had visited here, pride that the High Sheikh had seen something in him to educate him alongside his son, that he trusted him, an orphan, with state affairs.

He felt no such pride today and thanks to the woman splashing in the pool, no peace either. All he needed to do was close his eyes and he could imagine her slender shoulders dipping into the cool waters, could imagine her hands pushing away that inky dark hair, could imagine her lithe legs kicking through the water.

A moment's fear stilled him at the deceptive depth of the oasis on one side. Did she know how to swim?

Cocking his head to a side, he listened but only heard the smooth swish of water and her clean strokes.

The sand shifted under him, but he pressed on, knowing the path very well. The sky was lit orange with the setting sun, but until the orange orb set, the heat would not relent.

Neither would the knot in his stomach.

He'd had the perfect moment to ensnare her earlier. There had been such desperate longing, such a raw need in her gaze before she had shied it away from him.

It was a vulnerability he had never seen in Lauren, not after that first day in the situation room. He realized he preferred her glaring at him, questioning him, rather than that shattered light in those eyes.

Because, somehow, it had made him feel responsible for her. And not just her physical well-being. He had wanted to crush her in his arms, he had wanted to tell her that he would do everything and more that Bashir had done for Salma. That he couldn't wait to see his child suckle at her breast.

Anything, he would have done anything to bring back the smile to her mouth.

And it was the very force of that need that had stayed his hand.

When he knew he couldn't have her as his wife, it was all he'd been able to think about.

And now, now that marriage to her offered him the reins of Behraat, the advantage he needed over the High Council, now he was hesitating.

Why?

He withdrew his sat phone from his jeans pocket and made a call, leaving himself no room to back out.

"Tell me how the Dahab treated you."

Lauren had just finished her dinner when Zafir came back into the tent.

One glimpse into his face told her he was serious. "I was brought meals and snacks at regular intervals, called when Salma needed attention."

"Did you agree to accompany them?"

"Yes. Salma…lost a lot of blood. Ahmed refused to leave my side so I said okay." His frown deepened and fresh anxiety trickled in to her veins. "I've been thinking about that. Didn't Farrah get their message?"

His jaw set like concrete, he shook his head. "There was no message. You vanished and there was nothing."

"Wait, why wouldn't they—" She paled. If they hadn't relayed her message, that means Farrah or Arif or Zafir hadn't known where she was. "Why wouldn't they tell you?"

"The Dahab hate me, Lauren. And what Dahab believes, the other tribes follow. They figured out who you were and brought you along to send a message to me."

Fear fisted her throat but she spoke through it. "They were nothing but courteous to me." Shaking inside, she realized why he'd been so angry back in the tent, why he had held her like that… *He'd been worried about her?*

No, she couldn't be foolish enough to think he'd been worried about her.

His unborn child was a different matter. "They hate you…why?"

"I represent their disgrace, their shame." He clutched his nape, a show of vulnerability she didn't think he was aware of. "My mother was from this very tribe. She defied their rules and lived with my father while he was married, became his mistress and bore me out of wedlock. Which turned all the tribes against the state.

"I spent the first twenty years of my life thinking I was a mutt the sheikh took pity on. Suddenly, Crown Prince Tariq, who had been my friend for as long as I could remember, hated the very sight of me."

"He'd discovered the truth?" she added, her chest aching. He sounded matter-of-fact yet she knew the scars were bone deep.

"Yes. But it took my brother's abuse of power, utter ruin of tradition and duty that finally forced the sheikh's hand." Bitterness carved lines into his beautiful face.

"Rashid, the sheikh, very cleverly, reared me into a faithful, dutiful pawn of his and there I was, to the shock of the nation, the new heir, blood of my father."

"Then why were you in New York?" She understood the truth the moment she asked. Finally understood his anguished wait.

"Because Tariq didn't like all the power being snatched away from him. He put Rashid in a coma, bought off half the High Council and exiled me under penalty of death. Attacked the Dahab again and again, making their very mode of life untenable. Threw the nation into civil war and riots.

"I was waiting for the right moment to take back control of the city."

"Your mother…did you know her?"

He shrugged, a hardness that she hated settling into those angles. His answer when it came sent a painful exhale through her, so unexpected it was. "I don't remember her, if I ever knew her. Apparently, she was weakened after I was born and died soon after.

"The Dahab didn't want me and my father, for reasons of his own, had Arif put it out that I was an orphan he picked up off the streets.

"And you…" He uttered something raw in Arabic. "You got in the middle of it all."

"All I did was…" Lauren searched for the right words, "do my duty. I might not be the ruler of a nation, but I owe it to anyone who needs medical attention."

The words came automatically, as the horrific reality of her actions dawned on her. He hadn't known his *mother or father* growing up and she had hidden the knowledge of his child from him.

Suddenly, Lauren could see beneath the power and duty that he wore like a second skin, to the loneliness, the dark anger, the self-imposed isolation around him. And the hard man he had become to overcome everything his childhood had imposed on him.

Would he ever forgive her?

She'd betrayed him at the deepest level with her ignorant actions. And that guilt made her raw, defensive, unbalanced. "How would I know, Zafir? How would I know what I'm stepping into if you treat me like a prisoner, a mistress, and *now a brood horse*? Unless you accept that I have a role in your life, as much as you'd like to put me in a box and lock me there?"

His gaze stayed on her, thoughtful, almost open.

She pressed on, feeling as if she was taking a step into some unknown, without seeing a way forward.

Her relationship with her parents had always been transactions. If Lauren was a good girl for the summer at her aunt's, they would let her visit them in Morocco. If Lauren got good grades, then she could spend Christmas break with them in Paris.

Even the friends she'd made at the hospital, she'd always kept them at a wary distance, afraid of letting anyone close. But now…one of them had to take that first step. One of them had to clean the slate and start over.

"Can we try to be friends, Zafir? For the sake of our child?"

Silence beat in tune with the thud of her heart.

Slow amusement dawned in those golden depths, sending her system into stunned shock. One tip of that sensuous mouth tipped up, carving a crease in his cheek. "Brood horse, Lauren?"

A strange sound—a combination of a horrified squeak and an outraged gasp fell from her lips. "That's what you get out of the whole speech I just gave you?"

"So do we have a *breeding program* in place after you deliver this one?"

"You did not just call…you've gone mad," she flushed as he folded his hands in exaggerated patience, his mouth twitching. "A breeding program? Really?"

His jaw was rough with stubble, there was tiredness in the lines of his face. All she wanted to do was wrap her arms around him, to tell him that she understood him a little better now, that she understood the pain he hid so very well. But he wouldn't welcome her sympathy or her gesture of affection.

All he'd ever wanted, could ever want, from her was only one thing.

"If you're the brood horse, that makes me what? Your stud?"

The twitch of his mouth was infectious, the light in his eyes irresistible. "My very own Arabian stallion?" she said. He raised a brow in that infuriating way that he did.

His mouth finally curved into a full, breathtaking smile while her nerves thrummed at the sudden change in his demeanor. She understood why he had been worried and angry even, but now he was joking…

No, he was flirting with her. How? Why? Was he seducing her with that smile and those awful puns?

"I asked for that, yes?"

She exhaled long. "I seem to cause you—"

"I understand why you jumped in to help this time," he said, cutting her off. "I'm also willing to accept that you made an ill-informed and wrong decision with the right intentions. But you have to promise me that you won't take any more unnecessary risks."

Her ire rose at his autocratic tone. But since her new motto was to set aside her needs and insecurities for the sake of her unborn child, she said, "Anything else that Your Highness is willing to cede?"

"Behraat's political clime is changing. If I curb your freedom, it's because your safety—" He raised a hand when she opened her mouth, and continued, "and not just because you carry my child, is important to me. I would not have you hurt in any way, Lauren. Ever."

She folded her hands, willing her heart to stop racing. Never had she heard that raw emotion in his tone, never had such simple words held such sway over her. "Is your offer to reevaluate our situation after the baby's here still valid?"

"There will be no need."

Shaking her head, she glared at him. "You promised."

"Come here," he said in a curiously flat, nonthreatening tone.

He meant to touch her. That intent in his gaze was like a tug at her senses that she found herself swaying to the balls of her feet. "No."

Something hot and needy detonated in his gaze. And it took everything she had to not scuttle away like cornered prey.

He took one step toward her and she instantly sidestepped. "I think you have a subconscious fantasy of me chasing and capturing you, Lauren."

Heat tightened her cheeks. Being chased by Zafir, being wanted by him, needed by him…it was a crazy fantasy she'd already indulged in, all right. That messed with her head far too often. "Zafir, I…" She faced him, ignoring her racing pulse. "I don't want to fight with you."

Another step closer. "No, *habeebti*, we won't fight."

"I don't want you to touch me either. There's only so many times I can pull the 'do what you will with me' routine."

Something almost like amusement glinted deep in his eyes. "All I said was to come closer. I'd like to see the changes my child is making in your body," he said in an exaggeratedly patient voice.

"And then, we can talk? Like adults," she rushed over her words as he loomed over her, "adults who're going to share a huge, life-changing responsibility," his hands covered hers and tugged her, their legs banging each other before he steadied her, his scent luring her in, as she continued speaking, "who both want the best for their child and…" soundless pants fell from her mouth as his hot gaze seared wherever it fell, "who would never, *ever*, force their child to pick sides."

And then she was shaking from holding herself back and his hands moved down her shoulders gently, whispering something in his native language, something tender. Oh, how she wished she could understand the words falling from his lips before he gathered her to him, his palm resting at the base of her back.

Warmth uncoiled in her lower belly.

Finally, after what seemed like a lifetime of waiting on the edge of a knife, one hand moved to her hip and the other to her abdomen.

His chin dropped to her forehead, her heart thumping so loud in her ears. She hid her face in his chest, felt the beat of his heart under her cheek. A harsh breath fell out of his lips and she felt his powerful frame shudder all around her while his palm moved softly. "This is the most precious thing I've ever experienced in my life," he finally said in a hushed, husky tone that sent shivers down her spine.

At least, that was not a lie, Zafir thought, his heart bursting with emotion.

"Please, Zafir, let me go," came Lauren's hoarse whisper. "I can't... I can't breathe."

A muscle jumped in his cheek as he looked down at her, but he leashed the possessive need that flared through him.

She looked tired and sleepy, her wild hair only half-dry. He wanted to burrow deep under her skin and never emerge.

"Dealing with you is like trying to contain a sandstorm."

"I'll not say or be sorry for upsetting your life. Not when—"

"Not when the result is this baby, yes?"

His hand moved up her back, traced the line of her shoulders, settled at her nape in a possessive hold.

Now that she was going to be his, he realized he couldn't

contain his excitement. And not because of the languorous desire that hummed through his veins. But for the first time in his life, he felt something different, something tender and yet equally disconcerting.

"You love the baby so much already?"

"Yes." Her hands tightened around his middle. And he swallowed the tight fist in his throat. "More than I've ever loved anyone."

Stark and beautiful like the desert, the truth of her words resonated around him, filling him with a joy like no other. "I apologize for my harsh words to you."

He heard her breath catch, and then even out. She knew what he was talking about.

He would give her everything he possibly could, he decided in that instant. For everything he couldn't, didn't know, how to give.

Finally, the stiffness in her shoulders eased and he could feel her relaxing against him. The brush of her slight belly against his abdomen sent his breath hurtling through his throat. "I'll forgive you if you forgive me."

"Already done."

"Zafir, whatever the future—"

"Become my wife, Lauren."

Shock propelled Lauren out of his arms. "You're..."

Joking...she'd been about to say but the word disappeared as she looked at him.

Without a hint of shadow, his gaze gleamed golden. Every line of his face said he'd made up his mind.

He wanted to marry her. God, he would be her husband...

The very word felt strangely exciting in her mind, so possessive, and so irrevocably final. For she knew in her very bones that Zafir didn't make the decision lightly.

Shivers spewed in her muscles. And they were as much out of excitement as they were out of fear.

"I would not joke. My anger from the past clouded my judgment until now."

"Because you don't want the same fate as you suffered for our child?" Of course, that's why.

Clasping her hand with his, he pulled her close. "That's what made me think of marriage, yes. But it was just the spark that ignited it. It is right for us in so many ways.

"If I had acknowledged my disturbing propensity to forget all rationale and judgment when it comes to you, I'd have realized where this was heading long ago."

Her heart threatened to shove out of her chest, so hard and loud it thumped. She didn't need love. She herself barely knew it. But that he would make this commitment to her, it made her blood pound in her veins. "Somehow, I don't think it's a compliment to be associated with low judgment."

"That is all you will get out of me," he quipped and her mouth went dry.

"What about Behraat? About me being an American and not fitting in your world... What about all that virgin bride stuff and alliances that will bring..."

What about you and me, the question came unbidden to her lips.

But there was no *just them,* she told herself.

Those two months in New York, that had been stolen time.

Until it had changed both their lives forever.

Clasping her hand tight in his, Zafir said, "You pay too much attention to the palace gossip, Lauren. I thought you above that kind of thing." Her pulse raced under his thumb. "Have you ever heard any of that from my mouth?" When she shook her head, he nodded. "The Sheikha cannot be susceptible to rumors for there will be many who'll want to sway you to their side," he said, arrogant confidence dripping from his pores. "In any case, I will train you in our ways."

She scrunched her nose at him. "I'm not a pet to be sent off to training. Nothing will make me into the kind of wife or the woman Behraat will expect me to be, Zafir."

His large hands were now on her shoulders, his breath feathering her face. "Your life will change in a number of ways, but I'm confident that you will handle it all. Independence is one thing, Lauren. Marrying the Sheikh of Behraat, another."

Hand tucked under her chin, he lifted her head up until she looked at him. Pressed his mouth to her temple, "I need you, Lauren. Unlike anything or anyone else in the world."

Everything within her, every urge she had ever repressed came out to play when it was this man who looked at her as if she was his sanity, as if she could calm him, as if she could rebalance his world.

That he needed her had always been her downfall.

She took his hand in hers. "This will work only if you promise me one thing, Zafir."

Don't ask me for the truth, Zafir thought.

Don't force me to lie even more, the ones he'd already told scouring him.

Something resolute filled her face, chasing away the hesitation that came before it. And he braced himself and suddenly he knew why he had hesitated so much.

This incredibly delicate, infinitely fragile slip of a woman had power over him.

He'd already indulged himself for far too much when it came to her.

She made him want to be a better man, to risk things he didn't possess while his duty chained him, forever weighed on his soul. She made him wonder and speculate about, for the first time, life outside of being the sheikh's favorite orphan, beyond Rashid's son, beyond Behraat even.

She made him want to reach for the impossible.

"I need your fidelity, Zafir. I'll face anything if you—"

His breath shuddered out of him. This was a promise he could give and keep with no effort. He wanted no other woman like he wanted her. Once they were married, he would have Behraat, he would have the woman he wanted with an insanity and he would have his child.

For once in his life, he would have everything he could ever want. As long as he could forget that it was all built on a very small lie.

"I have not touched another woman since I came to your apartment that night, Lauren. And I will not touch another ever again." He didn't like that she needed his reassurance in it. That she didn't know what kind of man he was.

But like she had rightly said, he hadn't let her know him.

He saw the relief in her gaze and traced her cheeks with his knuckles.

A warm smile curved her lush mouth. Stepping onto her toes, she anchored herself on his shoulders and pressed her mouth to his stubbled cheek. The effect of that soft mouth was instantaneous—a searing brand.

Her words whispered at his ear felt like both a blessing and a curse, a vow that he felt to his very soul. "Then yes. I'll marry you, Zafir." She smiled against his cheek. "And I'll try, to the best of my ability, to be an…interesting wife."

Laughter bubbled up out of his chest. His hands sunk into her hair, he turned her to him.

The minx was laughing. Tightening his fingers, he buried his mouth in her neck and licked the fluttering pulse. Just the way that drove her crazy.

She smelled like sun and desert and warmth and desire, all rolled into one.

Too weak to resist, he pulled her to him until every inch of her thrummed against him. Hard and insistent, his erection pressed against her belly. "I see that you're not promising to be a biddable wife."

Her low gasp, the way her hands sank into his hair, his control barely held on. "That would be a lie, wouldn't it? We both know I won't be a *good little wife*. And I'd hate to start our marriage with lies."

He jerked up and released her. Her smile dimmed and he shuttered his expression.

With light movements, he touched her lips, pressed a quick kiss to her cheek and wished her good-night.

He'd almost stepped out when she called his name.

A frown tied her brow and wariness clouded her dark eyes. And in that moment, Zafir knew he was taking a momentous step, one he could never erase. A strange kind of weight settled on his chest.

"You're leaving?"

"I promised myself I would never make you feel cheap ever again. That means staying out of your bed until you're my wife and I have every right under the desert sun to be there."

He left without waiting for her response. Little time, he had very little time to get over this strange anxiety in his gut.

Little time to indulge in the foolish notion that he was committing a wrong.

He was marrying a woman carrying his child and bringing his country together again. He should be celebrating with a primal roar.

CHAPTER NINE

A MERE TWO weeks later, in which she saw her fiancé one single time for the space of one measly hour, Lauren Hamby married Zafir ibn Rashid Al Masood, the High Sheikh of Behraat in an outrageously extravagant but traditional ceremony in the great hall of the Behraati palace with guests ranging from distinguished state members from all over the world to stone-faced, bearded High Council members who wore their disapproval like a shield to any number of Behraatis, all of whom viewed her with a tangible curiosity.

The flowing, turquoise creation made of satiny silk that had been picked for her fell to her ankles in a traditional, not-hugging fit and hid her bump quite well. For which she would be forever grateful.

"The Sheikh of Behraat, Lauren? What about your scorn for a life that's only about ambition and power? In the face of that lifestyle, you've forgotten your petty complaints?" her mother had said over the phone, throwing Lauren's old words back in her face.

"It's not like that, Mom," she had said, for her own benefit as much as her mother's.

Then she heard the muted whisper of her father's voice and then her mother was saying, "Wait, he's marrying you because you got pregnant? Did you get the *nikah* contract checked out by a lawyer, Lauren? If he marries another woman later, because, *believe me*, these fantastic cross-cultural marriages burn out in a blaze as soon as the lust dies down…and their council, whatever it's called in Behraat, will want a Behraati sheikha, what does your child get? If he's a boy, is he going to be named heir?" She had continued in that vein while Lauren had felt nauseous.

Nothing about what her feelings for Zafir were or his for her, if he treated her well or if Lauren wanted her mom by her side for the first time in years.

Of course, they were too busy on diplomatic assignment to attend the wedding even though she told them of Zafir's offer to fly them back and forth within days in his private jet. And even after years of hardening herself against their disinterest, it still hurt that when the wedding organizer inquired about her family and friends attending, Lauren had nothing to say.

It had been the same evening that she had seen him in the ensuing two weeks. And he had brought the very contract that her mother had gone on and on about, for her to sign.

Too stunned to string two words together, she had stared at him. And he had replied that it was a tradition.

Once the lawyer had begun explaining what it entailed—allowance money, enough for Lauren and three generations after her to live quite comfortably—and she had gotten over her shock, she had abruptly stopped him and requested that he leave.

Zafir, who'd been sitting in a corner of the room, his attention on the tablet in his hand, had jerked his head up, his gaze pinning her to the spot.

"You're not well?"

At her silence, he had walked to her. Tension had tightened the skin over his cheekbones. "Lauren?"

She had no idea why she'd mentioned it at all. Only that it had been eating away at her since her conversation with her mother.

Only that there was this infinitesimal, gnawing ache in the pit of her stomach every time she found herself alone.

Nerves, she had told herself. The very landscape of her life was changing, on top of the usual pregnancy hormones, Farrah had said when she had betrayed her worries.

"My mother asked if we were including anything about custody and such stuff…in the contract," she had said, her heart in her throat.

Sunlight filtered in through the high, vaulted ceilings, the stained glass puncturing it into a myriad of colors. And yet, Zafir was like the cold frost in the middle of it. "What other such stuff?"

Perfectly courteous his question might have been but there had been such a dangerous, almost forbidding quality to his gaze then. A hardness that had forcefully reminded her of how ruthless he could be when he set his mind to it. As if the seductive, easy charm he had worn that day in the desert had been a mask.

As if she had suddenly morphed into that stranger who was only good for one thing again in his life.

"I don't know," she had mumbled, her own words leaving a bad taste in her mouth. "Stuff like what would happen to my…" A muscle tightened in his cheek, she splayed a hand on her belly, seeking reassurance from the tiny life inside her, "—our child if you married again and had children by another woman. About where we would live and…"

"Are you saying you need these…" his mouth curled with disgust, "clauses included in the contract? That you wish to discuss such…things?"

Distant and distrustful, this version of Zafir made her feel as if she didn't know him at all, as if she was, once again, risking everything for this man. There was nothing of the man who had asked her so tenderly to marry him.

But she was the one who had started the…horrible discussion.

"I…just…"

The tension in the room became so thick that she couldn't even breathe, couldn't even get her thoughts to cohere. Couldn't understand why she was pushing this when it hurt her just as much as it disgusted him.

Though he stood close enough now to touch her, he very carefully didn't, which was a lash enough, because, even in anger, he'd always touched her. "If you require these things written in a contract, then there is—"

"No," she had finally said, finding the very thought of him with another woman bile-inducing. "I want trust. I want respect. I…hate thinking about it like this."

The hardness had relented in his gaze. "I'll not begin it by putting threatening terms and conditional clauses, with the assumption that it will fail. I intend for this marriage to last forever. This is the only time we will talk about such things, Lauren. Do you understand?"

Tears that had threatened all week had finally spilled over onto her cheeks.

Relief, shame, fear—too many emotions squeezed her chest tight. But she met his gaze square. "Yes. But if your council doesn't accept me and they force you to marry a Behraati girl…"

Determination pulsed in his very expression. "They will accept me and you and our child. I left them no other choice."

And in that moment, Lauren realized how many of his own demons this man had faced, still faced, every day. How honorably he did his duty by those very people who constantly questioned his rule.

The powerful arrogance in his words had unbalanced her, rubbed her raw more times than she could count but it was the only way he knew, the only way he could rule.

It was the only way he had taken what was his. And she understood it just as she understood the sense of isolation around him.

The light behind him outlined his wide shoulders, the leanly sculpted chest clad in dark blue, and tapered waist and those tough, hard legs encased in jeans. Lauren blinked at the swirling possessiveness, the almost atavistic urge that filled her to mark this proud man as hers.

To make sure the world knew that he was hers and hers alone.

One hand on her shoulder, he'd swiped a tear from her cheek. "You didn't want to have this conversation any more than I did, did you?"

There was no hesitation in her body's response to him even as her mind sometimes resisted him. She swayed toward him, seeking the cocoon of his embrace. He held her lightly, the warmth of his body a teasing caress.

She sniffled and swallowed her tears. "No."

Tipping her chin, he'd studied her. Then his frown turned into an outright scowl. "Your phone call with your mother...that's where this began."

She shrugged.

"Are they coming to the wedding?"

"No."

"That's what upset you?"

"No, I had a feeling that would be their answer." And she had known.

The disappointment, the loneliness, they were all lessons she had learned after years of silent tears and bitterness but in the end, she had learned to deal with it.

Had poured everything she had into caring for those who could barely afford medical care, to serve people who didn't call her needy, or emotional.

High school and college graduation, her twenty-first birthday, the day she had received her first job offer...she had done fine without her parents at all the milestones of her life. She would do fine this time, too.

Acknowledging that had always given her a sense of

control back and it did now. Forcing a smile, she met Zafir's gaze. "Let's just chalk up this episode to hormones, please."

Instead of being relieved that she was giving him an out, he had frowned. "You hide the fact that she hurt you? Just from me or yourself, too?"

Her spine straightened, a defensive gesture that was coded into her blood. "I'm not hiding anything. And it's true. It's the hormones and this huge wedding that have just made me more susceptible."

"So she's not only not coming for her daughter's wedding but she planted all that nonsense in your head, knowing of your condition and that you're all alone here?"

She nodded, awed at how easily he had surmised the situation. "Something like that. But it's not her fault, Zafir." She didn't even know why she was defending her mom. "She's always been the pragmatic type—"

"Of course, it is her fault, Lauren. I'm glad she's not coming to the wedding, or she would have numerous occasions to upset you.

"In fact, I think you should not see her ever again. I will order the state secretary to inform your parents that their invitation to visit Behraat has been rescinded."

"What?" Lauren didn't know where to begin. "First of all, you can't just rescind an invitation, Zafir. That smacks of arrogance."

"I'm the ruler of Behraat. I'm entitled to arrogance."

Her mouth twitched, her breath went all wonky from trying not to laugh. She wanted to kiss him for making her laugh so easily. And she had a feeling he had intended it. But she refused to be railroaded into anything, even though she was never going to discuss her marriage with her mother ever again.

She sighed, realizing she had to fight his autocratic dictate for the principle of it.

"Second, you can't just decide that I won't ever see her again. Or anyone else for that matter."

"Why would you want to? It is clear that they care little for your happiness and well-being. And you're not in a condition to deal with stress like this. Nor will you while I have something to say about it."

"They're still my parents, Zafir. Your father didn't even tell you you were his son until he needed a better crown prince. And yet, here you are, doing everything you can to hold Behraat together by its seams."

She thought he would get furious with her for bringing up that subject. At the least, tell her she wasn't allowed to bring it up. Or withdraw.

Instead, he seemed thoughtful. And that he let her in just that much made her miserable day a thousand times brighter.

"It's ingrained in me, in my very blood that I must do everything I can to ensure Behraat's prosperity. My father needed no big gestures or promises of wealth to earn my loyalty.

"He molded me into his weapon with mere words. I've never met another such great orator. I would attend classes during the day, train with the palace guard in the evenings, but the nights…they had always been my favorite part of the day.

"For he would summon me to his parlor when he was ready for dinner. He would tell me stories of great battles, tales of warrior men who gave up everything for their nation, for their tribe, of armies marching into battle for freedom. And a nine-year-old boy who has no family… he begins to breathe those stories. Begs to hear one more, swears his loyalty, his very blood in exchange for one more.

"To survive, he needs to believe that he's part of something much bigger than his concerns. In the end, there's nothing else left of him except trying to make the tale into reality."

A tremendous sadness filled Lauren for the boy he'd been, for the flash of raw longing she glimpsed in his eyes. And a burning rage for the man who'd so heartlessly turned him into this…this man who believed that there was nothing to him than serving Behraat.

That he was nothing more than a tool to be used for his country. That there was no reason or need for him to want for anything more.

"Zafir? Whatever you believed then, it's—"

"It's a conditioning I can't defeat in this life." Absolute, implacable, his gaze warned her to not try, his belief an impenetrable wall she couldn't breach.

And how she ached to reach him…

"But in your case, I'm here to change it. So I forbid you from even speaking to her."

"Forbid?" She should have been furious, yet Lauren could only laugh. Could only marvel at how easily he had turned the whole thing around on her again.

Walking around the sitting area, she poked him in the chest. "You can't *forbid me* from stuff. In fact, we must remove it from our marriage dictionary. I'm going to be your wife, Zafir, not your servant."

"Marriage dictionary?" His eyes had turned molten, humor lurking in their depths.

"Yes." She held out her fingers and counted them, "Forbid, order, train etc. Can't be in there."

His gaze swept over her face, her breasts barely hidden from that overpowering male gaze in a thin, cotton henley, already feeling heavy and achy. Settled on her mouth. "Do I get to add some words to it, too? Like things I've begged for but was denied in those two months? Like a—"

She swatted at him, laughing and giggling, knowing how his wicked mind worked.

He sighed dramatically and every cell in her sang with dizzy joy. "What is in this dictionary then?"

"Laughter."

She had no idea when he had moved close enough that her breasts rubbed against that hard chest. She shuddered just as a growl rumbled from his throat. "I like the sound of that, *habeebti*."

She placed one hand on his chest to feel his heart and clasped his cheek with the other. "Affection. Respect."

His arrogant head bowed as if in reverence, his shuddering exhale caressing her face. She had the strangest feeling that he was hiding his expression from her. Hard shoulders relaxed under her tentative touch. His fingers crawled around her nape then.

Finally, his molten gaze bore into her, lingering over her mouth. "Surrender?" he asked and she shook her head.

"No 'surrender'. Comfort. Care. Friendship."

Deep satisfaction glinting in his eyes, he rubbed his nose against hers. "Seduce?"

"No seduce. Cajole. Kiss. Need."

He rubbed his mouth over hers, and she moaned. "I think I'm getting the gist of it, *habeebti*," he whispered against her mouth.

Holding on to him because she was afraid she was melting on the inside, Lauren spoke against those soft yet thoroughly masculine lips. Evening stubble rasped her flesh, making her whimper with want. "Yeah? Try it then."

"Marriage. Commitment. Forever."

Just as he stole her breath with his words, so did his hot, hungry mouth on hers.

Resistance, imagined or real, was an alien concept. She might have squeaked at the influx of such delirious pleasure and he took that opportunity to swirl his wicked tongue around hers.

Her heart was still racing from the promise in his

words, her belly tightening with such fierce feeling she thought she might burst with it.

Every time she thought she had a measure of him, he went and toppled her all over again. Made her need him on such a visceral level that she came undone by his words, his smile, his touch. Joy made her want that much hotter, bone-deep affection made her need that much deeper.

She had never felt such heights of dizzying joy or such a deep hollow ache as she did with this man.

Moaning in the back of her throat, she clasped his neck and clung to him by her mouth.

Until he pulled her hands off his neck, and whispered, "Only one more week, *habeebti*." Fire gleamed in his hungry gaze, his breath a harsh rhythm in her ears. "And if you get upset again because you didn't listen to me, I will put your mother in jail."

She sputtered and he pressed another hard, hasty kiss to her stinging lips. And then he was gone.

"Marriage. Commitment. Forever."

She had seen him only that once in the exhausting week and Lauren clutched those three words to her every time she felt as though she was sinking in the spotlight leading up to her fairy-tale, fantastic wedding that had Behraat and the rest of the world take notice of her.

She had never imagined her wedding day, having had only one disastrous relationship by twenty-six, much less on such a huge scale, and as the days blended into a flurry of activity, Lauren felt scared, isolated, inadequate and craving Zafir's company once again.

The palace staff in an upheaval over the upcoming wedding, even Farrah had kept their daily appointments to a minimum.

Exotic flowers and exquisite silks, diamond jewelry and

designer dresses, there was no end to the treasures Zafir bestowed upon her.

And in addition to the army of staff that catered to her every breath, she also now had a secretary whose job was to school her in everything social—mostly at what state ceremonies she could open her mouth and at what, which was 90 percent, she had to look poised and beautiful and ornamental for the sheikh.

"I will train you in our ways," he had told her arrogantly. And through those two weeks, she would have even taken his arrogant, imperious behavior if it meant she got to see more of him.

Abdul, her newly appointed secretary, she realized within two days, was adept at manipulating the truth to suit Behraat best. He had coached her intensively for an interview, the only one required of her, with a female journalist of a huge media channel. But when Lauren had sat down to watch it, her jaw had fallen to her chest.

The bits and pieces of responses that Abdul had fed her had been manipulated into a cohesive whole that told how Zafir and she had fallen in love with each other while he had been in exile, waiting to serve his country, how she had come in search of him thinking him dead, and how having found her again, the sheikh hadn't been able to wait to make her his sheikha.

It told of how a plain, hardworking nurse from Brooklyn, New York, had befriended their sheikh, fallen in love with him and now, had been transformed into the sheikha fit for him and his great country.

Lauren hadn't known whether to laugh or cry or take offense at being described as some kind of mouse who had unwittingly befriended a lion, and subsequently, transformed into an elegant deer?

Because levelheaded as she'd always been, even having been exposed to her parents' glittering, high-society life at an early age and turned her back on it, her wedding and all it ensued was on such a grand level that even her head could turn.

Could buy into the fantastical love story that the palace whispered it to be around her. Could delude herself that Zafir was marrying her because he couldn't bear to part with her rather than because it was the best thing for the situation they found themselves in.

But it was a commitment they had made and she was determined to give everything she could.

The morning of the wedding, minutes before she was due in the lavishly decorated great hall, she had seen Farrah and Huma standing in the corridor waiting to greet her. She'd barely embraced them when she saw David and a couple of her friends who had worked with her in the inner-city clinics.

Zafir had contacted David and the rest of them personally, Alicia had said with awe in her voice. Of course they had to come to see Lauren become the sheikha of her own nation.

Her chest ached as their words sunk in.

He had not only comforted her when she had been upset but had contacted her friends on her behalf. Domineering he might be, but Lauren was afraid he was slowly stealing bits and pieces of her very soul.

Beyond her friends from the States, another small group of men and women stood in the last hall. With Salma and Bashir at the front, Lauren realized it was the Dahab. Ahmed, standing close as always, had grinned at her stunned face, told her they had traveled to the city to stand witness to her wedding to their sheikh, to wish her happiness in her marriage.

Between Farrah's admonishments that they were getting late and Alicia's wicked whispers about Ahmed and the 'fine quality' of Behraati men in general, Lauren felt anything but alone.

In this strange country and between people she had only met for a few weeks, Lauren felt loved, cherished, and thanks to the dark, breathtaking man whose gaze swept over her with a possessive desire as she reached the great hall, utterly wanted.

Once she had repeated the vows that she had practiced, Zafir had nodded at the small group that had stood to the side of the hall. "Fans of yours, sheikha?"

Warmth filling her from the inside out, Lauren resisted the urge to plaster herself all over him. It was a losing battle, she realized as she studied his rough-hewn features, that generous mouth and the long bridge of his arrogant nose. "My tribe," she had finally said.

And he had smiled.

Before she knew it, they were joined together as man and wife in front of God and the people of Behraat and then she was whisked away to a feast unlike anything she had ever seen.

After two hours of raising sparkling water, picking at her food and thanking a host of dignitaries from around the world, her smile began to droop and her shoulders ached. The three-inch designer shoes that she had cooed over now felt like torture devices on her tired feet.

His hand around her, Zafir instantly held her as she toppled. Last she had looked, he had been walking around the room, greeting and meeting men she couldn't even remember the names of. That he had appeared by her side so fast…her breath shook.

Long fingers held her right below her breast and she felt branded, feeling his touch through her dress all the way to her skin. "You're ready to drop."

She saw the hunger in his golden gaze, felt the tight tension in his body, heard the hiss of his exhale as her hip brushed his front. Legs wobbling, belly tight with need, she said, "I'm sorry, it's just been a long day."

His finger landed on her mouth, while he signaled to someone behind her. "Don't apologize. I will see you tonight." He bent his head and whispered, "Get some rest, yes? It might be late but I'll be there."

Sparks of heat spreading to every limb, Lauren nodded.

She followed the contingent that seemed to be her shadow now.

No matter, she decided, because all she wanted right then was to escape from her own self, much less face the man who was slowly but inexorably imprinting himself on her very soul.

CHAPTER TEN

BY THE TIME Zafir had dealt with the numerous council members and state delegates, and the tribal chiefs led by the Dahab's chief, and arrived at the oasis, separately from Lauren, darkness had fallen like a thick cloak over the encampment.

He was glad he had sent her on earlier because his negotiations with the chiefs had gone on and on. And he had, eager to finalize the agreement he wanted to reach with them and loath to disturb the fragile peace, let half his wedding night pass by.

Not wanting to disturb her in case she was sleeping, he had the pilot land the chopper a mile or so from the camp.

The desert sky glittered with stars as he walked, the wild, crisp scent of the night driving his blood to pound faster in his veins.

Victory was his. For the first time in his life, he felt like he belonged to the Al Masoods, like the conquering warrior in those stories.

He had secured his rule of Behraat, had secured its return to a path of progress. Trade agreements could be renewed now that half its population wasn't trying to rip the other half apart. Excavation for oil could begin again in lands that had been occupied by the tribes.

He had done everything an orphan who had been thrust into power could have done.

And his prize was in that huge tent set just a little apart from the rest of the encampment, the path to the entrance flanked by a row of lanterns.

Tonight, he belonged in that tent, truly, with his wife. Even his father's wife, banished to the fortress in the old city could not contest his place here.

The wind whistling through the sands, the dark desert sky, and the harsh, unforgiving desert, he was a part of this land finally. And it filled every inch of him with a profound joy, an unquenchable fire.

He acknowledged Ahmed and another guard with a nod. She wouldn't like that they were so close by, the errant thought dropped into his head. Not for what he had on his mind, he thought with a smile.

But he wouldn't dismiss them. Not when her safety was paramount, not when he was hovering on the knife-edge of desire, his rationality and the civilized veneer like the slippery sand under his feet.

Before his next breath, he was standing inside the tent, at the foot of the vast bed. Numerous lanterns were lit all around the room and he wondered if she had been afraid of the pitch-darkness that was a desert night.

There she lay, *his wife*.

Still in the turquoise dress that had so lovingly hinted at those lithe curves. She slept on her side, the silk scrunched up to her knees, displaying toned calves.

Deep red henna swirled over her feet and hands. She was marked like that for him, he thought with a primal possessive urge like he had never known before.

His breath coming in short bursts, he devoured the sight of her. Her hair haphazardly framed her face, a mirror of the spirited, independent woman. The bodice of the dress dipped at her chest, her folded arms pushing up the globes of her breasts.

Need ripped through him, for the first time in his life, leaving him absolutely unraveled on a level he didn't understand.

Shedding his long tunic, he left his cotton trousers on. Much as he couldn't wait to feel her silken flesh against all of him, he didn't want to spook her when she was in such a deep sleep.

Slowly, he lowered his body onto the bed, shifted to his side and gathered her to him.

Mumbling something, she came to him, pliant and soft in a way she never was when she was awake, her dainty fingers drifting over his abdomen. His shaft tightened painfully and a groan burst deep from inside him.

Purring like a cat, she tucked herself against him, the scent of roses and her skin a sensory heaven. He hissed out a breath, the brush of her thigh against his sending shafts of heat through him.

Ya Allah, he had forgotten how fragile she had always been. Constantly pitted against that tough, self-sufficient exterior she presented, the delicate bones of her body and lithe curves made him feel like a hulking brute.

The remembered feel of her tight heat the first time he had gone to her apartment…desire was a roaring beast within him.

Yet, she had always stood toe-to-toe with him.

And now she was even more delicate, he thought, his gaze drifting over her curves, and going to the small, just-visible swell of her belly.

She was finally, irrevocably his. She carried his child in her womb, wore his ring on her finger.

His child and his wife, *his* in every way there was.

His, in a way no one had ever been.

His, in a way no one could ever take away from him.

The whisper of rustling clothes brought Lauren awake from the deep slumber she had fallen into. She blinked and sat up, the flickering light of lanterns illuminating her surroundings for her.

It took her a few seconds to realize she was at the desert hideaway, and that it was…*her wedding night*. Pushing her hair away from her face, she grimaced at the tangles. She had fallen asleep the moment her head touched the pillow, and had neglected to take her pins out. Wondering what time it was, she looked up.

Standing at the edge of the bed, his sparsely haired, lean chest bare, a white towel slung low around his hips, there was Zafir.

Her husband, hers to hold and obey and…love.

Her vows came back to her word by word, but panic was only a mild flutter in her chest now.

Faced with such potent masculinity, knowing that this powerful man had pledged his fidelity and respect and his body to her, everything else paled in significance.

This time, she was prepared for the burning flame of her own need, of the blast of heat that punched low in her belly.

Golden light bathed the musculature of his chest, delineating every ridge of tightly roped muscle and sinew. Droplets of water clung to his skin, skin that she knew would feel like rough velvet. Muscle and sinew, he was breathtakingly gorgeous and he had never been bared to her like this.

She must have made a sound—a needy whimper, because he turned around then.

Tawny eyes met hers and she gasped aloud.

A savage light filled those golden depths. He looked fierce, dark, like one of the warriors he had told her about, as if there was a well of some bright fire inside of him that lit him from the inside out. Power and confidence radiated from him in waves.

Fear of some unknown crashed through her, and she clasped her hands together to stop their shaking. This was ridiculous. She knew this man, but the reassurance rang hollow.

"Zafir?" His name was an entreaty on her lips, a soft intonation. As if she could tame whatever it was that clung to him like a second skin. As if she could call forth that veneer of civilized sophistication that she'd always known was only skin-deep.

The hand in his hair with a towel stilled and he looked up at her. A thoroughly possessive light glinted in his eyes as his gaze lingered over her brow, her nose and finally rested on her mouth.

"Did I wake you?"

Clutching the voluminous folds of her dress, she pushed her feet to the ground and stood up. "No. How long have you been back?"

Another rough tumble of his hair and then the towel went flying into the corner. "An hour, maybe." Catching her look around, he said, "It's almost dawn."

"It took so long?"

Powerful shoulders rose as he shrugged. "Go back to sleep, Lauren."

She licked her lips to moisten them. "No. I'm fine." An infinitesimal shudder racked the tense line of his shoulders. "You went for a swim in the oasis in the middle of the night? You must be freezing!"

"I needed to cool down."

That matter-of-fact statement hung in the room, sparking into life a simmering fire.

He was half-naked and she was drowning in silk and yet, she felt as if she was the one utterly bared to him.

Reaching him on barely steady legs, she stilled. The skirts of her dress fluttered against his legs. She thought his mouth must have twitched at how strange she was acting, but when she looked into his eyes, there was only that deeply disconcerting hunger again.

He was just as still as she was, waiting for what, she had no idea.

Breath hitching in her throat, she tried to smile. She had no idea where the sudden tension was springing from, why she felt as if she was meeting him for the first time. How a ceremony could drench them in a strange kind of intimacy. "Did everything go okay?"

He frowned.

"At your meeting with the High Council?"

"How do you know?"

"Ahmed said it was a meeting of all the tribal chiefs and the council members, a meeting unlike he had ever heard of or seen before." Hardness inched into his face until the planes jutted out starkly. "That none of the staff had any idea that they would even be arriving for the wedding. That they hadn't set foot in the palace, much less the city for so long. That you brought this all about. Is that true?"

"Yes. They will not contest my rule anymore."

Short, clipped and with a warning. That she didn't heed. "That's fantastic. Ahmed said—"

An edgy smile, more a snarl, touched his lips. "Ahmed, it seems, is a raging gossip and probably half in love with you, yes?" He seemed so utterly displeased that for a second it was like looking at a stranger in the same skin. "Maybe he needs a tougher assignment where he's not mooning over my beautiful wife and speculating on state matters?"

Heat tightened her cheeks as she strove to make light of his claim. But there it was again, that tinge of barely civilized hint to it. "Please don't do that. Ahmed's... *infatuation*," she said, and was relieved to see the tight set of his mouth relax a little, "is perfectly harmless and nothing I can't handle."

And then she was wondering why she had said please. Wondering what subconscious instinct made her want to appease him rather than argue like she had always done, what unnamed, wild thing inside him she recognized today, of all days.

At his raised brow, she flushed again. "I like him. He's young and friendly and—"

"You can't socialize with the guard, Lauren."

If she didn't know such a thing was impossible, she would have thought him jealous. But jealous meant caring on a different level and speculating on his feelings or lack of them meant she'd have to face what she wanted them to be.

She injected steel into her voice. "And not prone to prejudice or judgment, like other members of your staff is what I mean," she finished, thinking of his mentor, Arif. Although, for the first time since she had seen the older man in the trade center that day, his rigid features had relaxed when he had looked at her at the feast today.

Grudging acknowledgment, maybe.

"Tell me about the meeting, about their impression of me."

"You don't need to concern yourself—"

"Don't say that. You don't have to protect me from… the worst."

"As your husband, that is one of the job requirements, *habeebti*," he added archly. "Whether they be old, distrustful council members or your mother or even yourself that I have to protect you from."

She bit her lip, hating the insecurity that balled up in her throat. Normally, she would have closed herself off completely, barred any way she could hearing what some traditional, rooted-in-the-past old men thought of her. Not venturing where she wasn't needed, that had been her motto and her shield all her life.

Her parents didn't want her to tag along on a year-long assignment one year?

She'd made plans the next year before they could even reject her.

If she didn't give anything, there was no possibility of getting hurt.

But for the sake of her child, and for the sake of this man who had cared that she was upset, who had, while shouldering the burden of his volatile nation, still spared time to realize she must be feeling alone…

For him, she would face her fears.

She would not only face them, but she would never give him reason to be ashamed of her, she decided with a fierceness that was new to her.

"Why did they all show up in such force? To express their disapproval of me?"

"The Dahab approve of you and arrived to honor you. And the rest of the tribes follow where they lead." He shook his head, as if signaling to end the matter. "But I've had enough politics today to last me a lifetime, Lauren. I don't wish to discuss it anymore."

Commanding and absolute, his voice sent a shiver up her spine. It felt like dismissal. But something lingered in his face too, something that set a twisty feeling in her gut and she decided to let the matter drop. For now. "Okay."

Before she could turn around, one of his hands snaked up and caught around her nape, tugging her closer. The rasp of his hard chest against hers sent fire blasting into every nerve ending. Her lashes fell down and she dug her fingers into his shoulders. But even after his midnight swim, his skin was still hot.

"You're very submissive all of a sudden. Why?"

"Not submissive. Understanding," she corrected him, "and slowly learning to choose which battles to fight."

He pushed out a breath and his body seemed to tense up even more. "You're sure you've had enough rest?" he muttered against her temple. "I'll be gentle, I promise."

Low and deep, his words shot straight through to the core of her, leaving her writhing in her own skin.

"I fell asleep the moment—" The words barely left her before his mouth crashed down on hers.

She wanted to say she didn't need him to be gentle. She wanted to say that whatever it was that was burning inside him, she could see it. She wanted to say that she'd, *always*, want all of him—the tenderness and the passion, but also the harsher, tougher aspects of him.

The part that regretted a brother's death even though he'd made his life hell.

The part that hated the father just as much as the part that still, somehow, loved and grieved for him. Deeply.

The part that had been stunned that she'd come looking for him all the way to Behraat.

Even the part that had made him walk away from her as much as the part that admitted that what they'd shared hadn't been cheap.

All the parts that made him Zafir.

All of him. Always, she realized with a shiver.

But he didn't give her a chance to say any of that, and she was perversely glad because it was easier to surrender to the pleasure between them than face what she knew would change her entire life.

CHAPTER ELEVEN

HOT AND SLICK and expertly teasing, his wicked mouth was all she'd dreamed about in the past few weeks. The taste of him was erotic, the drag of his mouth righting her world, chasing away the silly anxiety, rocking through her with the force of an earthquake.

She wound her arms around his shoulders, hanging on as he drove her mindless with his desperate caresses.

The light in the room was only a soft glow yet she felt as if there was an explosion of color, sensation and dizzying excitement around her. Attar of roses and some wild fragrance from the desert and the scent of Zafir's masculinity, it was a cocktail she got drunk on.

Silk that had been soft when she had worn it this morning now rasped roughly against her knotting nipples. The lace of panties rubbed against her wet folds.

She knew him, her body screamed with a roar of delight.

She knew this mouth, knew those deep strokes of his tongue, knew the bite of teeth that grazed her lip, not so gently, knew the hoarse grunt that fell from him when she tangled her tongue with his. Knew the hunger and passion he kept buried beneath his isolation, knew the heart of him.

And then he was pushing her back with his large body, back toward the bed, all the while his mouth devoured hers with rough, almost desperate strokes.

With his hands on her hips, he braced her fall onto the bed. Stood at the edge and looked down at her with molten gaze. "Tell me what you're thinking."

"That I wish I could use telekinesis to make that towel drop," she drawled, pushing to her elbows.

"If my wife wishes it…" he said and then the towel was falling to the floor.

"Oh…" Fractured and desperate, the sound fell from her lips as she studied him to her heart's content.

Washboard abdomen, tapered hips, rock-hard thighs and the thick-veined length of his erection that rose up toward his belly…her womb tightened remembering the pleasure he could wield. She smoothed her hands down her belly as if she could calm the need clamoring inside of her. As if control of any sort wasn't a big, fat lie around him.

Powerful sheikh or not outside of this tent, here he was, quite simply, her man. Panty-meltingly gorgeous with a body honed to hard strength.

I will touch no woman ever again.

"You're all mine, Sheikh," she said, boldly raking a fingertip down one rock-hard thigh.

His hands drifted to her ankles and clasped one and softly slid her up the bed. He climbed up after her, pinning her to the bed by her dress, his hips snuggling between her legs, his weight on his elbows.

Muscles gleaming in the flickering light, copper-hued skin stretched tight over those pectorals, he leaned over her like some dark warrior claiming his prize.

He pulled back to his knees. One calloused hand found her ankle, moved up her leg, palm down. "Your mouth, that's what got us into this trouble in the first place, yes?"

The soft skin behind her knee, the sensitive skin of her inner thigh, from the line of her hip to the seam of her silk panties, those fingers learned all of her anew. It cost her several breaths to find her voice, unsteady and hoarse as it is. "So, what, this is all my fault?"

Her thighs squeezed as his big, calloused palm pressed

farther. Gaze greedy and hot and all kinds of wicked, he watched her reaction. As if he enjoyed her coming apart as much as he enjoyed making her.

Head rolling back, shoulders coming away from the bed, she moaned as his palm covered her mound and pressed. All of her being pulsed under his hand, wet, and aching and desperate.

His other hand snuck under her dress and then he was pulling those wisps of lace down with one hand and pulling her down on the bed to straddle his legs.

While she watched hungrily, hanging upon the knife-edge of desire, he bared her lower body while her dress stayed snug over her aching breasts. Her legs, her thighs and the slick, drenched folds of her womanhood, all of her.

And looked at her.

"Beautiful," he muttered in a tight, clenched voice, the glow from the lanterns highlighting the sharp sweep of his cheekbones, the sensuality of his lower lip.

After all this time, Lauren felt the heat rushing and pooling under her skin, flushing her with color. She hadn't been a virgin, but nothing had prepared her for his brand of pulse-pounding, soul-baring kind of passion in New York. Without promises, without the usual, useless rituals of dating, without her knowledge even, he had stolen a part of her and imprinted himself on her.

No wonder she had followed him across the world.

"Zafir…please…"

His hand on her knee stopped her when she tried, too late but still, to shield her sex from his hungry gaze. And by the glint of masculine satisfaction in his gaze, he knew it. He liked that she trusted him, that she was putty in his hands while he did as he pleased.

He parted her sex with a possessive, intrusive, yet arousing touch and stroked her.

A hoarse moan left her mouth.

"Wet...you're so wet for me. How do I take this slow?" He sounded almost angry as if his loss of control was her fault. As if he didn't thoroughly relish having her drenched in the desire he created in her with one mere look.

Lauren saw the deft flick of his wrist before she felt his long fingers inside her.

A million nerve endings in her groin went ballistic.

Sobbing and moaning, Lauren gave in to the fire he set inside of her.

Her body arched off the bed as he slicked his fingers in and out while his thumb pressed down at the swollen nub crying for his attention. Again and again, he pressed on that bundle while she writhed under his touch.

And just when a tremor started in her lower belly, he withdrew his fingers.

She cried, so close to release and yet so far away again. Her fists landed on his shoulder, his chest as he knelt over her. Opening her eyes, she met the dark, male heat glittering in his.

A golden flame, an incinerating hunger.

"I can't wait any longer," he said, through clenched teeth, his hands roughly pushing the silk folds out of his way. Almost apologetic. "I should have known..."

Holding her hips down, he pushed into her wet heat with one firm stroke.

Their mingled groans ricocheted in the tent.

Twisting the sheets with her fists, Lauren let her legs go slack. Even having known this intimacy with him, her slick channel was still not prepared for how big he was.

After six years of celibacy, she had flinched when he had entered her that first evening in New York.

Again now, she had to breathe, short, panting bursts, through the invasion of his velvet heat, brace herself for the raw, mind-numbing friction in the walls of her sex.

Skin damp, clenched muscles rock hard beneath her fingers, he exhaled. Something almost like regret lingered around his mouth as he touched her damp brow. "You're fine?"

"Yes," Lauren breathed and wiggled her hips. A fist of need twisted her lower belly afresh.

"Come for me, *habeebti*," he said, his fingers once again finding the swollen button of her sex.

Lauren curled her legs around his back as he pulled out and thrust again. Excruciatingly slow, he let her feel every inch of him, his fingers relentless in their assault still.

She was sobbing and begging now, pressing his back with her legs, urging him to go faster. Going mindless at the release that hovered just beyond her reach.

Every muscle in his face pulled tight over his features, his jaw looked as if it was set in concrete. She knew his body, she knew what he liked when it came to sex, what drove him crazy. That he needed to go faster, deeper, rougher.

Heart murmuring to a halt, she realized that he leashed himself.

It was the only time she had him, the man in the center of the island he made around himself, the man he was beneath his dedication and duty to Behraat and she was damned if she gave that up because he thought she might break.

"You can't hurt me."

A vein flickered in his temple, his gaze filled with a feral hunger. Hunger that he denied himself.

She tried to shift under her him, but he locked her with his fingers on her hips. "Zafir…" she panted, furious that he would deny her. "I'm pregnant, not an invalid."

"I know that." She pushed a damp lock of hair from his forehead, something filling her chest. "But, do you know how fragile you feel to my rough hands?" Another slow thrust followed by their mingled groans.

She drew her nails down his back, the heated hiss of his breath goading her on. "Shield me, if you must, from the entire world, but not from you, Zafir. Never from you," she said, and then she traced the line of his rigid spine, dug her fingers into his taut buttocks. "I swear to God, if you treat me like this, ours will be the shortest marriage in the history of—"

His mouth took hers in such a carnal kiss that she felt thoroughly ravished. "You will learn to not threaten your husband, *habeebti*," he whispered, before he dipped his tongue into her mouth in actions mimicking his lower body. "And you'll definitely not talk of leaving me again, ever. Yes?"

"Harder, then, please," she murmured at his ear. His skin was rough silk as she licked his shoulder and then pushed her teeth in.

A hoarse grunt fell from his lips, before he clasped her jaw and crushed her mouth with a savage ferocity that burned her. There was no gentleness to him now, no semblance of control.

He was the man that had made her embrace insanity with a smile, that had made her wild with one kiss. That had made her leave safety behind and walk into fire.

Tilting her hips, he thrust deeper, faster, pushing her on and on… Until there was only him and her and the spiraling want between them…

Lauren screamed as she came in a shattering explosion of pleasure and sensation. Her lower belly quivered, her legs so much mush, her sex pulsing and shuddering with the waves.

With a guttural growl, Zafir followed her, keeping his weight off her even as his powerful body bucked and shuddered above her.

* * *

His breath coating his throat like a fire, Zafir looked at Lauren.

Brow damp, her breathing harsh, she was shaking.

His thighs still tightening and releasing from the aftermath of his explosive climax, he looked down the length of her. The scent of sweat and sex clung to the air they breathed, an explosive mix that he drew greedily into his lungs.

He saw the pink impressions his fingers had left on one hip and cursed. One layer of lace that fell over the turquoise silk beneath, he assumed, was ripped along the seam. Feeling himself harden again, he pulled the dress down all the way to her ankles.

A shuddering exhale left him, his chest feeling as if it was caving in on his heart.

Moving away from the bed, he found a washcloth, dunked it in a pitcher of water and came back to the bed. Gently, he snuck his hands again under the wreck he had made of her dress. She flinched when he separated her legs.

Ice filling his veins, he froze. Then he rolled his shoulders and searched for her gaze. "Lauren? You said—"

"Zafir!" Eyes, wide in her narrow face, locked on him. Her lashes cast shadows onto her cheeks, her skin damp. "I'm just…embarrassed, that's all."

Relief unlocked his wrist. Smoothing his palm over her belly, he continued again and gently cleaned her up.

Because they had never lingered like this after sex before, he realized. Because every time, after he had taken her, he had left.

The only time he had actually stayed at her apartment had been when she'd had the flu.

Because, every time, he had told himself it would be the last time.

Because, from the moment of his father's announcement to an outraged Tariq and a stunned council, he had not been just Zafir. Or was it even before that when his mother had given him birth.

The way Rashid had raised him, it seemed it had been inevitable.

But now, he needn't walk away.

Because she had helped him carve a small compartment in his life, for her.

He liked that—the permanence of something in his life, the freedom to be himself, even if it was in the very confines of this one relationship.

Freedom by binding him to her, that's what she had given him.

"You're smiling," she said then, and she was smiling, too. Lovely mouth trembling, dark black eyes glowing.

His heart crawled to his throat.

It was one of those perfect, precious, rare moments, he just knew it, even though there hadn't been very many in his life until then.

"I plan to be there when you give birth, Lauren. I plan to cut the cord and see my child enter this world. This," he said, gesturing to the cloth, "it's nothing, *habeebti*."

"Yeah?" she said, something low and tender in her tone more than challenge.

"Yeah," he replied, with a smile. He thought he saw a flash of wetness but she blinked and looked away.

Getting off the bed, he cleaned himself and then washed up. He felt her gaze on his back and turned.

She looked utterly breathtaking on that vast bed, the bodice of her dress clinging to her breasts.

He hadn't even undressed her, he realized now. Just shoved her dress up and out of his way before plunging into her. Even the chilly waters of the oasis hadn't cooled him down.

He had been high on his victory, drunk on his own power, as she had blamed him once.

He had meant to take it slow, to savor the long night, but the moment he had touched her, found her ready for him, he had lost any semblance of will.

She wanted it just as much as you did, a part of him whispered. And she never pretended otherwise.

She had never feared him or his passion. Not before she knew who he was, not after.

Something inside him, something that feared that he would heap a world of hurt on this fragile woman, finally calmed.

This wild heat between them, Lauren wanted it.

Lauren always chose it, always chose him, he realized with a leaping feeling. And for the first time in his life, he could give back what little he could.

He returned to the bed and pulled a thick rug over their bodies. Traced the upper swell of her breasts and felt her shiver. "I'm a fool, *habeebti*, not that I would admit it to anyone but you."

"How so?"

"I ignored these glorious breasts."

"Hmmm…no arguments here," she said, sinking her fingers into his hair and pulling.

She didn't do it gently either. Then satisfied, she moved those long fingers down his forehead, over the bridge of his nose, his mouth, before settling over his shoulders again.

Then she petted him some more.

He lay still, silent, shuddering at the possessiveness in her touch, submitting to this woman who was slowly stealing into him. "Zafir?"

"Yes, Lauren?"

Her thickly fringed gaze fell on him, then shied away. She was hesitating, and instantly, he felt something in him twist and brace.

Against her? Against what she would say?

Was it fear, he wondered, trying to hold the curious feeling swirling through him. It was the same sensation that had shot through him when she had so boldly blurted out that their marriage would be short if he didn't...

Buried deep inside her, straining to not use her body roughly like he was used to, he had growled back at her.

He, who had finally achieved everything, could he fear what this mere slip of a woman could say to him? And what she could do?

She roughly pulled his chin up to meet his gaze. The uncertainty there pushed away his own jumbled thoughts. "What is it?"

The flush was receding from her cheeks, but her mouth was swollen. From his rough kisses. "Focus, will you?"

This time, he laughed. "I am focusing. You're the one hesitating. Which is as strange as a rainfall in a desert."

She didn't negate him. And his heart pounded harder in the thick silence.

"I've...you..." She sighed, licked her lips, rubbed one thumb over his stubbly jaw and began again. "I've been confused, overwhelmed and sometimes a little lonely these past weeks... But then..."

She pulled his hand to her cheek, and then kissed the center of his palm. The tenderness in her gaze unmanned him. "I would do anything to make this marriage work, Zafir. And not just for the baby. But for you and me."

He didn't know what to say in return.

It was what he had known she would give in return for his commitment, it was what he wanted of her for years to come, and yet the strength of her conviction, the courage it must have cost her to say it to him, shook him from within.

And because he didn't know how to stop it from shifting and splintering something inside of him, didn't know how to form a suitable response, because it was a promise the likes of which he had never known in his life, he bent and captured her mouth with his.

He worshipped her with his mouth, his hands and his body while her soft declaration took root in his veins, his cells, in his very blood. Like the roots of a gnarled tree that stood proudly in the courtyard of the palace, planting itself tight and deep within him.

The expression in her eyes, the joy in her smile, the tenderness in the way she touched him and kissed him, as if she couldn't contain it anymore, as if it was bursting out of her every breath, it haunted him long after she fell asleep and he extracted himself from the bed and watched the dawn coat the sky a myriad of oranges and pinks.

And then, just like that, in the space of one night, no, just a few hours, he felt as if he had lost it all. Before he had even grasped it properly yet.

As if all that he had achieved was so little next to that one small declaration from Lauren, which he hadn't earned.

Through the following four days that he allowed himself to spend with her, through his return to the palace, through every breath he took, her words haunted him.

It haunted him until he couldn't breathe for the weight of it, until every time he saw Lauren, it felt as if he deserved her, her open smile, her affection, less and less.

Until every word of hers felt like a small lash in his skin.

But this was the life he had wanted all along, wasn't it? The life in which he had everything?

CHAPTER TWELVE

AFTER FOUR DAYS of tasting paradise at the oasis, Lauren and Zafir returned to the city and the palace.

They had woken up before dawn one morning, and watched the sunrise together over the sand dunes. Swam in the pool while moonlight glinted off their skin. She had glutted on dates and figs and thick cakes, between fever-ish bouts of lovemaking during which she had, hopefully in a final way, proved to Zafir that having his wicked way with her was in no way harmful to either her or their grow-ing child.

That it was very much what she needed.

They had exchanged college stories around a campfire in the evening. His, always working toward his goal of becoming a member of Behraat's state affairs, and hers, building a life that nurtured her need to help, away from the sphere of her parents' high-society life.

During the day, he'd been gone for a few hours, visit-ing different tribes before they migrated deeper into the desert, he'd informed her. Needing to recover from their long, busy, sweat-soaked nights, she was all too content to nap in the tent and stay away from the blistering heat.

It had been pure bliss and all Lauren wanted was to stay there forever with Zafir, cocooned away from the world.

But just like in New York, real life—full of schedules and meetings, and government and state dinners—awaited both of them this time.

She had barely showered, changed and inhaled more food when Abdul had appeared at the entrance to her suite, with a host of social appointments and a load of advice. Even before Farrah had appeared to check on her.

So Lauren fell into a routine, pushing back at Abdul at some things and bringing down Arif's stone-faced wrath on her head, sometimes letting them mold her into what they needed the sheikha to be. Refused point-blank on some issues.

She did miss her old life. But she knew that to be a symptom of her resistance to change, to teams of strangers taking over her life.

Her career, however, was a different matter.

She had put in years of hard work to get her nursing degree, and then long night shifts to gain experience and reputation.

All she did now was spend her days watching her team fight over which designer she should wear or which charity she should grace with her presence. It felt as though she, Lauren, got smaller and lost in the huge tsunami that was Zafir's life and Behraat.

To her shame, she'd even burst into tears a couple of times, but she decided to give herself a break and chalk it up to pregnancy hormones rather than call herself a coward.

Zafir, she decided, had paid enough all his life for Behraat. He wouldn't lose her to it too; whether he knew it or not, he had her.

And just like that, she felt a little in control of her life again.

So what if she chose the social engagements that were closer to her heart like women's issues and girls' education rather than spending another afternoon with the old shiekha and Johara—who wore a brittle smile on her face while the old woman bitterly complained about Zafir, short of calling him a murderer to Lauren's face.

Lauren however didn't mistake the older woman's hatred or the younger woman's veiled malice to be anything personal. That she had married the man who had usurped their son and husband respectively was bad enough. But that she was also an American and pregnant on top of it was a pill they just couldn't swallow.

When the old woman, however, began ranting about Zafir's mother, Lauren had walked to the door, called Ahmed to escort her guests out and returned to her bedroom.

That whole day, she had spent thinking of Zafir's mother, her defiance of her own tribe, cutting away every tie and living in shame with a man who hadn't even married her.

Had she loved Rashid so much then?

If only she could spend an evening with Zafir, just the two of them. Asking for one evening in two weeks was not petulant, she'd told Farrah who refused to stick her head into anything remotely marital.

The numerous public occasions and state dinners during which they saw each other and smiled and barely exchanged two words didn't count.

Neither did the nights when he came to her, sometimes at midnight, sometimes even at dawn.

The first night, three days after they had returned, Lauren had seen him earlier at a state dinner. She had worn a royal blue creation with long sleeves and a conservative cut that didn't declare her pregnancy blatantly. A Russian oligarch, who was interested in investing unholy amounts of money in Behraat, who apparently was very fond of New York City, was the guest of honor.

He had monopolized Lauren for most of the evening. The man's icy blue gaze lingered far too much over her body but Lauren had just smiled and nodded.

And none of it had escaped Zafir's notice.

It had been past midnight and Lauren had fallen into a sort of restless slumber after retiring to her quarters.

Hardness and heat, the wall of masculinity behind her had woken her up. Smiling, she had purred and stretched into him, her body already thrumming with anticipation.

That luscious mouth of his had kissed a blazing inferno down her spine, pulling away at her wispy nightgown. One hand snuck under her and played relentlessly with her breasts, pinching and stroking her already highly sensitive nipples.

He'd remained silent, which was strange in itself for she loved all the words he used to tell her how much he needed her. It was only after he had teased her to a fever pitch, hurtling her to the edge of climax, after commanding her to lift her leg and pushing into her from behind that he had finally spoken.

Teeth had dug into her shoulder, sending a spasm of sensation down her spine. "I don't like the way the Russian looks at you," he'd said, in a low voice that had been ripe with warning. "And I don't like that I don't like it."

Lauren had closed her eyes, breathing roughly, trying to sift through his words.

That she was not to make light of it, shouldn't argue with him on it, was clear. That it wasn't her that he doubted. That he felt so much at all. That he'd needed to claim her in the most carnal and intimate way before he could bring himself to mention it.

Tilting her head back, she'd sought his mouth, pulled the scent of him deep inside. "The investment and even more importantly, the exposure he brings to Behraat is not something you can turn your back on." The slight widening of his eyes made her glad she had read through the file her aide had prepared for her. "Neither can you hide me away because then it looks like you've noticed his interest and taken offense.

"The only remaining option, and the one that you despise is, pretending that you don't care, continuing to let him look at me like that until the deal with him is actually done.

"This is Behraat we're talking about, so there's not a choice, is there?"

He'd withdrawn and then thrust back into her slick heat, a darkness that scared her in his gaze. But even with her mind worried, still she had gasped at his skilled strokes and languorous kisses. Still, she succumbed to the need inside.

"Not only beautiful and smart, but such understanding too?"

She'd definitely known something was wrong then. Because his smile, it hadn't quite reached his eyes. And Lauren had a feeling that moment, that night hadn't been just about the Russian. "Really, Zafir, handling a few hours with one arrogant jerk who thinks he's God's gift to women is not that big of a deal," she'd somehow managed.

Something bleak had passed his eyes. He'd muttered something explosive in Arabic, pressed a kiss to her mouth and then began moving inside her again.

A couple of times, she imagined she'd glimpsed a shadow of pain in his gaze but then he would kiss her as though he couldn't breathe and she forgot all about it. Having learned so much about his childhood, she didn't expect some grand declaration of love from him.

His actions and his commitment to her and their child meant more than anything to her. The tenderness in his eyes when he glanced at her growing bump meant more than words.

But, her mind being the only place she had any sort of privacy left in her new life, she retreated to it often and there was no hiding from truth.

She had fallen in love with him. And the realization didn't come about like a flash of lightning like she had always imagined.

It crept up on her in the middle of a small gathering, one she'd had Abdul arrange, in cahoots with a reluctant Arif and Farrah, Ahmed and Huma and a few other staff that she'd been told had a friendly relationship with Zafir.

The small gathering waited in her quarters, both awkward and excited.

Please don't be distant, she'd been muttering to herself. *Please don't let this be a horrible idea that only pains him more.*

And then there he was pushing the wide doors open and striding inside with that prowling gait and they were all yelling, "Surprise!"

Thunder danced in his gaze.

The cheers they had practiced went from excited to a stunned silence as Zafir searched the crowd, his gaze still serious.

Finally, it fell on her.

Pulse thudding, somehow Lauren had covered the little distance between them.

Still, he stared at her, shock set into his features. "I was told you needed my attention urgently."

She didn't care for his tone. "I made sure it wasn't some super important meeting that we interrupted."

"But you made me think something had happened. To you."

"Oh…but, you can see, I'm fine." She rose up on her toes and kissed his unshaven cheek. Felt his lean frame tremble under her. "Happy birthday, Zafir."

His fingers snuck into her hair and pulled her closer.

Arabic fell from his mouth, like a clap of thunder. Within minutes, the room cleared out, leaving just them.

Stunned, Lauren turned back, swatted Zafir in the shoulder. "How could you?"

"Easily. I'm their sheikh."

She pouted. "They all wanted to wish you happy birthday and I'll have you know I went to a lot of trouble. It's not easy planning a surprise party for the man who has—"

She never finished her sentence because he picked her up. Her hands went around his nape, her heart thudded but she tried to keep the smile from her mouth.

"I wanted to be alone with my wife," he growled then.

Long strides carried her past the sitting area to the bedroom. He put her down on the bed with a tenderness that caught her breath. And then his hands were on her bodice. When the silk didn't cooperate, he ripped it with his hands, pushed away the silk of her bra and closed his abrasive palm against one plump breast.

"Zafir…" She threw her head back and moaned as he buried his mouth in her throat. Traced a searing path down her chest to her breast, licked the engorged tip. "Wait, I…"

"No, no waiting." Then his mouth closed over her nipple, licking and suckling, and then there were teeth. "Now, *habeebti*. I need this now."

A whimper fell from Lauren's mouth, her spine arching, her body bowing under the pleasure. Pulling her to the edge of the bed, he shoved her dress to her thighs, pulled her panties down and entered her in one long, smooth thrust.

Silk and steel, velvet hardness against wet heat, their bodies built up into a perfect rhythm, beautiful and raw, earthy and something out of this world, at the same time.

With soothing words, he bent her over his arm, and took her breast in his mouth.

Hands in his hair, Lauren rode him shamelessly, shuddering and splintering until they reached the peak together, and crashed down to earth again.

"I can't believe…" She flushed and hid her damp face in his chest, pulled in a much-needed breath and looked up again. "You were not supposed to do that."

His thumb brushing her cheek, he frowned down at her. "What? Not touch my lovely wife on my birthday?"

"No, turn the evening into…this. I mean, yes, but we could have waited."

"And you know when it comes to you and being inside of you," he said, nibbling at her throat again, "that I can never wait."

Looking down, she flushed, and held the edges of her torn bodice up. "I wanted to spend an evening with you. Outside of bed." It was hard to sound miffed when he looked at her with such hunger in his eyes. "Talk about what's going on with you and such. I know the weight of Behraat lies on your shoulders, but I…"

"What?"

"We see each other at those ghastly dinners, and then you make love to me in the dark of the night. It feels like… I'm trying so hard not be a petulant wife, Zafir… I… If there's something on your mind, *about us*, or anything else, I have a right to know."

Shielding his gaze away from her, Zafir tucked her head under his chin and held her tight. His heart still thudded from the fact that she'd arranged a party for him. "Lauren…you're so much more than I ever expected to have as a wife, *habeebti*." This, as he was learning every day with her, was the absolute truth. "As predictable as it sounds, I've just been busy, preoccupied."

"Okay," she said readily enough but Zafir wasn't sure she was convinced.

How had one small manipulation become such an impenetrable wall between them, he wondered. How had giving them both what they wanted turned into this ever-growing chasm?

What the hell was wrong with him that he had everything he had ever wanted and he was playing with it like this? He knew, even as he acted contrary to it, that Lauren would never let him put her in one safe compartment, just because he didn't like himself very much right now.

This wallowing was a weakness.

A weakness that made him look away from her, that made him shudder at what he spied in her eyes. That made him wish he was anything but who he was.

And that was the kind of useless, helpless thinking that he despised the most.

That made her doubt that he was not happy with her, when she was the one perfect thing he'd ever held in his life, was unacceptable.

He had no reason to be not happy.

Shoving away the lead weight in his gut, he moved back from her, grabbed a cashmere wrap from the bottom of the bed and slowly wrapped it around her.

When she looked down, she was frowning, thoughtful.

And he felt a flicker of fear unlike he had ever known. Not even when he'd thought Tariq would execute him had it clawed through him with such intensity.

He took her hands in his and pulled her off the bed. "I shouldn't have ruined your plans, yes. You have cake, I presume?" he said, smiling.

Whatever doubts she'd had earlier, her gaze was clear now. And a little naughty as she raised her brows. "I had it flown in from a bakery in New York. German chocolate." She laced her fingers with him and tugged him. "You might feel faint once you taste it, so hold on tight to me."

He burst out laughing and went willingly. "Now I get it. This whole party was a ruse. You just wanted cake from New York," he teased.

Eyes glinting like the brightest opals, she smiled. "Okay, you caught me. But believe me, you've not had cake like this, Zafir."

He let her voice wash over him as she extolled the life-affirming virtues of delicious cake. Joy and fear were both his in that moment.

This woman could calm him and excite him, drench

him in warmth just as easily as she undid him. And there was nothing he could do about it. He couldn't lose her and stay the same, he knew with a certainty that made his gut twist hard.

She hummed "Happy Birthday" while he cut the cake and then brought a small piece to his mouth. He licked at her finger, the action instinctive, his need for her as natural as breathing and ever-present.

Pink tinged her cheeks but she pulled away. She served two pieces, handed him silverware and ordered him to pour coffee for both of them.

Took one bite of the cake between those imperfectly wide lips and moaned so sensually that he was instantly hard.

He took a bite himself and smiled. "How do I compete with cake?"

Zafir and she had just finished their coffee when his phone rang. About to complain that he'd promised her an uninterrupted evening, she caught the words just in time when she saw his expression.

Pulling the cell phone out, he stared at it. And then he clicked it on.

She saw shuddering shock, and relief and such pain in it that she reached for him instantly.

So much emotion, such anguish cloaked his features that looked as if they'd been carved into that mold. "Zafir? What's wrong?"

Slowly, his gaze focused on her. As if he had been far, far away from her. "My father…he is awake. And asking for me." His tone had a tremor in it.

"Six years… The last time I saw him, he'd declared to the council that I was his heir. He and Tariq were arguing, *screaming, threatening each other.* And when Tariq left with a murderous glance at the both of us and my father

turned to me, I told him I despised him. That I'd been better off as an orphan. And the next evening, he was found
collapsed in his room. His food was poisoned."

"Oh… Zafir…"

She wrapped her hands around his nape and pulled him
down to her level. Slowly, softly, she kissed him, pouring
everything she felt for him. Leaning her forehead against
his, Lauren clasped his cheeks. "Are you afraid?"

He laughed again, although it had a bitter tinge to it.
He didn't push her away and she was unbelievably glad
for that. "No. But I'm weak enough to wish I was anyone
but who I am."

"No, Zafir. This…pain I see in your eyes, this grief,
this love for a man whom you have every reason to hate,
your courage to do the right thing by Behraat, by me, by
your father, by everyone that falls in your sphere…this is
what makes you you, Zafir. And why I love you so much."

His eyes widened, his chin jerked back. As though she
had taken a swing at him. As though it was impossible,
even unacceptable for her to feel such a thing for him. As
if it was the worst fate he'd ever faced. "Lauren…"

"Why do you sound so shocked?" she said, determined
to hold on to her flailing courage. That he was so stunned
was not a bad thing, she reassured herself. "But this isn't
the time, right? While your father's waiting. So go see him."

Zafir never returned the night he had gone to see his father.
After waiting for a few hours, Lauren had fallen asleep,
still worried about him.

About them.

A furor of activity took place once it had become known
that the old sheikh was out of the coma. Not more than a
day had gone by where he hadn't had numerous meetings
with council members, Ahmed had told her when she'd
begged him for information.

All with Zafir present, she'd learned. Even the tribal chiefs were there now.

In between those long meetings, she had gone to see Rashid, too. The unresolved animosity between father and son, mostly from Zafir had rattled her. When his father had asked Zafir to leave them alone, he'd point-blank refused.

To which, Rashid had leveled him a long look.

Rashid, his gaze incisively intelligent, had quizzed her about her family, her life in New York. But couldn't really say much with his son watching them like a hawk.

Two days later, Zafir found her in the library, one of her favorite rooms in the palace. Dressed in a gray silk suit that lovingly draped over his shoulders, he was all business.

A team of aides and the ever-present Arif stood outside the door.

"I have a three-week trip to Asia," he said regretfully, after kissing her, right in front of the library staff and Ahmed.

"Three weeks?" she sounded dismayed, and for once she didn't care. She was tired of seeing those shadows in his eyes. Tired of wondering if he was pulling away from her. Tired of the constant ache in her chest. "You're not doing this to avoid me, are you, Zafir?" She'd no idea where she had found the strength to pose that question, this courage to put herself out there when it was becoming more and more obvious that it was the last thing he wanted to hear.

His mouth flattened. "I'm trying to get these long trips out of the way so that I can have an easier schedule when the baby comes. We'll talk when I come back. I promise, Lauren."

She had held on to him tightly, curbing the words that rose to her mouth, wanting to be given voice again and again. Locked away the wet heat that pricked at her eyes.

The depth of her feelings for him, the longing for him, it wasn't something she was used to yet.

"I've told my father," he said, "that he's to leave you alone while I'm gone. Don't let him bully you in my absence."

The next couple of weeks passed in a blur. Just as Zafir had warned her, Rashid had summoned her twice but she had found excuses both times. Not that she was afraid of him. She was more worried she would rip into him for Zafir.

Her first ultrasound was due in a few days and Zafir and she had argued over the phone about whether they should learn the sex of the baby. And when he laughed like that, when he told her that he couldn't wait to kiss her, everything was perfect in her world.

She'd just finished her yoga class and showered when Ahmed informed her that Salma was in the city and wanted to visit with her.

Thrilled, Lauren welcomed Salma with a hug. She took the chubby infant from Salma, and cuddled her. Farrah, who had stayed on to see Salma, translated between them.

Laughing, they chatted together happily. But when Farrah repeated something Salma had said, Lauren was confused. "I'm sorry, what does she mean, she's happy I accepted the arrangement?"

Farrah asked Salma to elaborate. Salma's response, translated by Farrah, "She says that her grandfather, the chief of the Dahab, made a promise to Zafir. In return for you saving Salma's and the baby's life, he would bring the tribes together, help Zafir unite them with state. As long as Zafir stopped following in his father's footsteps and married the nurse. With the tribes back in the fold, the High Council finally had to accept his rule."

Lauren stilled where she stood, a kind of numbness

spreading through her limbs. He hadn't even wasted an evening before he had proposed to her. And this was why...

Like everyone else in her life, she had only been secondary to his actual goal. Like always.

She slid to the settee in a shaking heap, her chest so tight that she couldn't breathe.

"Head down, Lauren. Between your legs," Farrah's voice sounded sharp, as if it was rolling in through a fog.

Breath came rushing into her in huge gulps and with it the sound of her heart shattering. She heard Farrah rushing Salma out and closing the door. Heard her call her name, her face worried.

But as she raised her head, and scrunched her knees up, all Lauren could see, hear, feel was Zafir.

"I need you, Lauren. Unlike anything or anyone else in the world."

He'd so cleverly laid out a trap for her without really saying anything, let her spin a story with his teasing glances and caresses and words.

Manipulated her into believing what they had was more. When it was not even the mere marriage of convenience she had thought.

Used her guilt that she had hidden the truth from him. Used their unborn child. Used her growing feelings for him.

Played the part of the charming, teasing man who was beginning to feel something for her.

All for Behraat.

She hadn't asked for the fantasy of it. She hadn't asked for him to tease her, and charm her and pretend as if he cared about her.

You're the fool, Lauren, something nasty whispered inside her head. *You've always been a fool for him, since the beginning.*

Again and again, he'd proved that only Behraat counted for him. It was only Behraat that had his heart.

Pulling in a long breath, she got up from the settee and told Farrah that she wanted to lie down.

Behind her bedroom door, she crumpled onto the bed, every inch of her thrumming with fury.

She couldn't bear to be here another moment. Couldn't bear this ache in her chest. Couldn't bear to live the rest of her life with a man who had, again and again, not only showed her how little she meant to him, but used her and their situation.

How could she ever trust him again? How could she trust herself, when apparently, she could spin a fantasy out of nothing?

Afternoon gave way to evening and she shivered at the sudden chill coming in from the balcony.

She splashed water on her face, changed her clothes, called Abdul and instructed him to arrange a meeting for her. Only one person would help her leave the palace, the city and Behraat without notifying Zafir. Without caring about bringing down Zafir's wrath.

She had to leave before he was back. Or she would never leave.

Worse, she would live the rest of her life, knowing that she would never have his love but crave it anyway, caught in a misery of her own making.

And she would not be alone in her misery.

Zafir checked his watch, calculated the time difference and then dismissed his staff.

Picking up his phone, he walked to the balcony of his forty-fifth-floor suite and looked out at Beijing. It was a damp, cold night and he itched to be back in Behraat, in the palace, besides Lauren.

Every time he closed his eyes, he remembered the

stricken look in her gaze, the tremble of her lips as she asked him if he was avoiding her...

Always challenging him, always making him wonder what else was there to life, what else he hadn't known, what else, first Rashid and then Zafir himself, had deprived himself of in life...

Like that impromptu birthday party.

Her cell phone rang a few times before she picked up.

"Hello, Zafir." She sounded groggy, tired, hoarse.

His nape prickled. Something prowled inside of him then, a knowing, a feeling of fear, of loss, of a wide yearning chasm.

Something was very wrong.

Even her hello sounded distant, full of a weight he didn't understand. He shouldn't have left her, the first thought pounded into him. He shouldn't have been avoiding her. He shouldn't have...

Lost his head over her in the first place? Shouldn't have let her weaken him like this?

Shouldn't have fallen in love like this at all.

Because now, she made him want to defy the entire world for her, she made him want to do the impossible just so he could be worthy of her love. She made him want to damn himself just so he could be with her.

The murmur of a male voice in the background pulled his attention away from what it seemed had been as inevitable as breathing. He pressed his thumb at his temple, took a long breath.

Then he heard Lauren's low answer and then the door closed again.

Ahmed wouldn't come into her bedroom, even if Lauren considered him a friend...

He still couldn't believe how easily she had his staff eating out of her hand, how easily she had integrated herself into such a different, difficult life. And she had done it with barely any complaint.

"Lauren? Are you sick?"

"No. I'm fine. The baby's fine." He heard her hesitate, the rustle of clothes, and then she cleared her throat. "I was sleeping."

"But you never miss your yoga class. Did something upset you?"

He felt her amazement, and his own, stretch tautly in the silence, an incandescent flicker in the darkness that he could sense was coming at him. Among all the million things that ran through his brain on a given day, he'd remembered that and hadn't even known it.

"Lauren?" he prompted again, and this time, he knew what it was that pulsed through him.

Desperation. Panic. As though he was sinking in the middle of the vast, stark Behraati desert, swallowed up by its great jaws like every other ruler had before him. As though after all his struggle, after everything he'd learned from Rashid and everything he'd been forced to learn since being thrust into power, he was somehow still empty-handed.

"It's early morning here, Zafir." Clear, cutting, she was in control of herself again. "In New York."

His breath punched out of him and his hand fisted by his side. A great, big roar began in his chest, crashing everything inside him into pieces, thundering its way out. But he swallowed it away. Like he had always done any emotion, any impulse, anything that would be detrimental to his dream, his rule of Behraat.

"And why, *exactly*, are you in New York?" He sounded edgy, rough and he didn't care.

"I left. You and your beloved Behraat."

He exhaled, his breath stuck in his throat like cut glass, every inch of him shaking, as if he stood cold and naked.

As if every ounce of warmth had leeched out of his world, never to return.

"Why?" he still asked. As if it could be some small, mundane reason that had prompted her to flee when his back was turned. As if he had been finally rendered into this weak, pathetic shell of a man who hoped for impossible things.

Everything inside of him clenched tight, waiting for her answer.

"You don't know, Zafir?"

Now, she sounded like the Lauren he knew. Like the Lauren that had brought such joy and light into his life, the Lauren that had made him think of himself for the first time.

Like the Lauren that somehow kept wrenching parts of him away.

"God, you looked into my eyes, you held me in your arms and you told me this was for our child. While all along…it was to cement your rule of Behraat." She sounded so angry and yet her voice shuddered. "You…lied about everything."

"No. What I did was try to do right by everyone. Just like you said. When the opportunity came, I grabbed it with both hands. It was unbearable for me to know my child would not know his or her place, just like me. Untenable for me to walk away from Behraat. Unbearable for me to…

"And then you…you made it all possible. For once in my life, I had a chance to have everything I had ever wanted. And I took it."

"You'll always put Behraat first."

Pushing a hand through his hair, Zafir tried to breathe through the knot in his throat. And for the first time in his cursed life, he asked something for himself.

"Don't ask me to be someone else, Lauren. Don't walk

away when we have something so good. Do not call it love and then wreck what we have with its weakness and its exalted expectations of sacrifices and grand gestures.

"Don't ruin it all because it doesn't fit your vague notion of what love should be."

Lauren felt the dark anger in his words like a whip against her skin. "I threw myself into this marriage with everything I had and more. I..." Tears threatened to steal away her words, her very will. "I even told myself that your feelings for me didn't matter. Not when you..."

"Then come back."

"But I'll always wonder what could take you away from me. When Behraat will make you choose over me and our child.

"What new political alliance and promise of power would be the thing that makes you decide it's worth more than us? It'll kill me, Zafir."

"Then you do not know me at all, much less love me. And the kind of reassurance you ask for, it's not in me to give." He sounded like the crack of thunder, angry and cruel and final, and it seemed to suck away the breath from her very lungs. "Your vow, your grand declaration...they are nothing but empty words, lines from a fantasy you have of what love should be.

"And I..." it trembled then, his voice and Lauren shivered, "I am the fool that I believed you, that I tortured myself every minute that I didn't deserve this thing between us...and you, that I hoped at all," he said in such a tired, empty voice that Lauren could imagine that dullness that would dim his golden gaze, the weight that would pull at his sensuous mouth, the tightness that would descend on those broad shoulders.

Lauren stared at her phone for a full minute before she realized he'd hung up.

And then, she cried. Big, racking sobs that had David inquire outside the door, tears that burned her nose and eyes and throat, shook her body, and hurt her head.

This wouldn't be the end of it, she knew. Not this argument between them or the last she saw of him. Not the last of the fire he'd made her walk through from the first minute.

Zafir wouldn't give up on this child they'd created and that wasn't a bad thing, she told herself, as if that could cleanse away the misery that sat like a boulder on her chest.

CHAPTER THIRTEEN

LIFE, OF COURSE, didn't come to a standstill, just because you got your heart broken, Lauren realized painfully over the next month. Twenty hours after Zafir had ended their call, a real estate agent had arrived with keys for her old apartment and a very betrayed-looking Ahmed after him.

"He banished me here, after berating me and four generations of my ancestors for losing sight of you, over the phone. For letting you leave. And now I'm to guard you here, in this crowded, noisy city. He should have just killed me," he said, despair high in his voice.

Lauren, feeling emotional and lonely and heartsick for Zafir and anyone remotely related to him, threw her arms around him. Ahmed's thin frame froze at first, and then slowly he patted her back awkwardly. The expression in his eyes, like deer caught in headlights, made Lauren laugh in the middle of tears.

"I'm sorry, Ahmed," she'd said and he'd nodded, understanding in his gaze.

With Ahmed's help, Lauren settled back into her apartment. When she'd asked him where His Royal Highness thought Ahmed was supposed to stay, he'd told her an apartment had been arranged for him, on the same floor of her building.

Before she could even make a list, a delivery service stood at her door, with milk and juice and fruits and steaming hot meals. Since refusing would mean talking to Zafir again, Lauren let herself be pushed.

With Zafir arranging her life to the smallest detail, even

a continent away, she felt as if she was in limbo, waiting for some slick, high-powered law firm to start custody proceedings.

A month passed while she played with the idea of going back to work, yet didn't, a month in which she hid from Alicia, because she couldn't bear to tell her the truth and make it even more real, a month in which she heard not a word from Zafir.

Even Ahmed, who accompanied her on her long meandering walks through the parks and streets, and compared New York to Behraat incessantly, carefully veered away from anything related to Zafir.

And the more rational and in control of herself she became, the more Lauren went over every look, every word, every touch Zafir and she had shared. Faced her cowardice in running away without even waiting for him to return, forcing him to offer an explanation over the phone.

But he wouldn't choose her over Behraat. Ever.

Did she want him to, she wondered as winter approached and the days grew shorter and she became less and less sure of herself.

Would that be the same man she had fallen in love with if he did?

Like a toll he had to pay for being loved by her? Was that what her love was—a transaction?

On another gloomy, chilly day, which made Lauren wish for the sweltering heat of Behraat, not that she would ever admit it to Ahmed, she returned from her evening walk when she saw the sleek, armored limousine idling at the curb in front of her building.

Her pulse racing, she shied her gaze away and made it to her apartment on the first floor. She had pulled a bottle of water from the refrigerator, panic swirling through her, when there was a knock.

Bracing herself, she opened the door.

The bottle fell from her fingers and hit the floor with a swishy sound.

Rashid Al Masood stood there, the corridor shrinking several sizes by his height. That sunken, unhealthy pallor was gone and she felt more than a little awe at his commanding presence, unbalanced and off-kilter at his golden gaze, so much like Zafir's.

"May I come in?" he said in a papery voice and Lauren, too shocked still, signaled for him to come in. He held out his hand toward a shadow that materialized into a man, took a file from him and then stepped in.

Fear beat a tattoo in her chest as Lauren's gaze fell on the papers.

Maybe he was here to ensure the termination of their marriage? Maybe he'd already found a new, better suited, bride for Zafir? Maybe…

Stop it, Lauren.

Zafir wouldn't do it like this. He wouldn't send a messenger, his father of all people, to end this between them. Not after everything they had shared.

But you've told him that all that didn't matter. That it was all a lie. That the one small thing he hadn't told her minimized everything else he'd shared with her, felt for her, showed her.

She sank her fingers into her hair and pushed at it, a strange fear gripping her limbs all of a sudden.

Some sort of sound must have escaped her because Rashid peered down at her.

"Do you require medical assistance, Ms. Hamby?"

"*I'm not Miss Hamby anymore.*" Her response was instant, defensive, like a screech of wind in the silence.

"Yet you're here, thousands of miles away when your place is by my son." Dry and derisive, his voice scraped at her nerves. "For six years I've been in a coma and little has changed in Western society's perception of marriage."

"You've no idea what happened between us. Nor do I owe you an explanation."

"I can see why my son indulged in this nonsense with you." His gaze lingered on her face thoughtfully, then shifted to her belly for a fraction of a second. "But that he lets you have this reckless freedom in this dangerous city when every minute of every day, you court the media's eye or even harm. I reminded him that you're his wife, that he should command you to be back in—"

"I'm not a possession, Your Highness."

"Is it my grandson's safety that you're so careless about?"

Fury rattled along Lauren's nerves. "You've no right to speak to me that way. And that it's a…" She slapped a hand over her mouth and glared at him. "I won't share that with you. Not before I tell Zafir."

Because she had broken their agreement and asked the ultrasound technician to tell her.

She'd waited for him to call so that she could share the news. Had been dismayed that he hadn't. Instead, he'd had Farrah call her and confirm that everything was all right.

As if he was completely through with her.

"Is my son aware that you know then?"

Shocked at how easily he'd manipulated her, she tried to corral her thoughts. "My child will not be yours to mold, Your Highness. I won't allow it and neither will Zafir."

He bristled at her reckless statement.

"You seem to be certain of a lot of things about a husband you have fled. In secret, with a bitter old woman's support, a woman that wishes him no less than a painful death. Do you have any idea the risk you took in trusting her with your child, my grandchild's, safety? Or how it torments my son, night after night, as if your reckless actions were his fault?"

"Stop it, please," she whispered, sweat pooling over her. God, what had she done? What had she turned her back on? "Just…tell me why you're here. Or leave."

Arrogant pride filled the gaunt crevices of his face. "All of Behraat is at Zafir's feet today, as it always should have been. Yet there is no joy, no pride in his eyes. You…" His gaze seemed to spear her, and with doubts eating away at her, she struggled to hold it. "…have weakened him, crippled him in a way I can't seem to fix. My son will not be brought down by a selfish, spoiled, so-called independent *American* who doesn't understand the first thing about duty and—"

"Maybe it's you who did that to him," she attacked, loathing herself as much as he seemed to. Because, the galling thing, the bitter truth was that he was right.

For a moment, her words suspended there in the room, like bullets stilled on their way to the target in some 3-D action flick before shattering away.

His eyes widened in disbelief but she didn't care anymore. Not when every cell in her ached to see Zafir and hold him. "Maybe it's time to stop asking Zafir to give more of himself to you and Behraat. Maybe if someone, for once, thinks of him, instead of sucking him dry in the name of duty, he'll smile and laugh again. Maybe what he needs is someone who loves him unconditionally for the kind, honorable, generous man that he is, then he will…"

And in her own desperate, impassioned words, Lauren found the truth that she'd been so blind to see. As if it was there all along inside her, clawing to get out.

A whimper fell from her mouth.

It was herself she'd never believed in.

For all her promises, she'd been waiting for a reason to believe that Zafir would abandon her like her parents had done, waiting for it all to fall apart. And the moment their relationship had been tested, at the first hurdle, she'd run away.

As if life and love were a fantasy she'd could dabble at, just like Zafir had mocked her.

That he'd chosen to unite Behraat didn't cancel out all that he'd shown her. Didn't corrupt all the promises he'd made her.

She buried her face in her hands, the scope of the damage she had wreaked a lead weight on her chest.

Rashid stood up and looked at her, a smug little curve to his mouth. As if victory was finally his.

"It is clear you were never right for him with all the nonsense you just spouted. His sheikha would understand his destiny and would not distract him." With every wrong thing Rashid said, Lauren could see the right path.

Both she and this insufferable old man were wrong, too absolute, too rigid in their thinking. And Zafir…he'd been walking that tightrope all along. From the minute he had met her.

"I suggest you have your lawyers look at the papers I brought. My son needs to put this…*episode* behind him. As for my grandchild, I'll—"

"No," Lauren threw back, straightening from the couch. She'd face this bully and a thousand more like him for Zafir. She'd prove her love a thousand times over to Zafir if only he'd give her another chance. Mind made up, she said, "I'm not going to sign a thing and you can't make me. And I'll tell Zafir that you were trying to blackmail me into cutting all ties," she added for good measure.

Rashid's stare was flat, derisive. Could have scorched her into ashes, if she let it. "You think my son will believe your word over mine? If you still haven't learned your lesson—"

"If you care anything for Zafir, if there's even a little

regret inside that political heart of yours about what you denied him for so many years, you'll take me to Behraat," she demanded.

Warning glittered in his eyes. "There's nothing but misery for you in Behraat. Zafir does not forgive." And in that last sentence, there was a crack, a deep regret.

"I'll take my chances," she threw back and slammed the door.

She quickly dialed her ob-gyn for an appointment.

She'd beg if that's what it would take.

Lauren had to wait eleven hours and twenty minutes after setting foot in the dusty, blazing inferno that was Behraat before she saw Zafir.

Through the ride in the armored, dark-tinted limo, Lauren saw little villages en route to the city between long stretches of rough road in between. Her pulse thudded when the high walls of the palace came into sight.

This was home now, she reminded herself resolutely, even as she felt daunted by the task ahead.

Only to be told by Rashid's nasally aide that she'd have to wait.

She'd eaten, walked a path on the rug, fallen asleep out of sheer exhaustion and jet lag, wanted to scream at the silence, had even wondered if Rashid hadn't somehow imprisoned her with no intention of ever telling Zafir again. But she'd been shown into her old suite.

A day of administrative affairs cannot be disturbed for one emotionally weak woman, Rashid had said before leaving her to his staff, a grim smile to his mouth.

Not Farrah, not Huma, not even Arif, it seemed knew of her arrival. Only Ahmed waited outside in the lounge, as much a prisoner as she because he'd refused to leave her side. Even when Rashid had commanded it. Patted her shoulder in encouragement in that awkward way of his when he'd realized what she meant to do.

She'd showered and changed into a sleeveless tunic and loose, flowy cotton trousers and once again, fallen into a restless sleep. Inky black night cloaked the room in semi-darkness and she wondered what had woken her.

When she checked the time, she was shocked to see she had slept for more than three hours.

She sat up and whimpered as a cramp twisted her calf.

"Should I call for Farrah?"

The room lit up in a blaze of lights and Zafir stood at the foot of the bed. Tall. Dark. Impossibly gorgeous. Heart-wrenchingly remote.

"How long have you been here?"

He shrugged, as if he didn't care enough to answer. And in that casual tilt of his shoulders and the dull glow of his golden eyes, Lauren knew she was walking a very tight line.

Throat tight and limbs shaking, she looked at his face bathed in the light. A deep well of emotion clamped her chest.

His dark blue dress shirt and black trousers utterly failed at masking that barely civilized air around him. Thick stubble marked his jaw and her fingers itched to trace the proud angles of it. He'd let his hair grow longer and it made his face even more narrow and gaunt. Dark shadows hung under his eyes and she wondered how long he'd been up for if Rashid's words were to be believed.

Undiluted power clung to him, like a second skin, and she knew now that it was both his weapon and armor, as much to rule and right Behraat as it was to keep everyone out.

And yet, he'd let her in and she had thrown it all away.

Dismay swirled through her, threatening to break her, and she wondered if she'd already lost him.

When she tugged her gaze to his, something in it made her mouth dry. "It's just a cramp. I should have walked around more on the flight."

She pushed the throw away and got off the bed. She stumbled, her legs feeling like noodles but straightened herself.

While he stood there unmoving, his gaze cold, his demeanor utterly unapproachable. As though there was an impenetrable fortress around him and he'd allow nothing to touch it. As though he'd buried himself deep beneath those walls.

"Zafir, I—"

"Is it advisable for you to keep traveling back and forth on such long flights whenever you please?" Those golden eyes fell to her belly, and she saw his mouth flinch before he skewered her again. "Have I given you too much credit in this as well, Lauren?" Taunt and threat, his honeyed voice could cut her skin. "Will you make a monster of me yet by forcing me to imprison you, *habeebti*?"

She flushed and searched for the right words. Which mistake did she start apologizing for? "I made sure it was all right for me to travel. You know that I would never take an unnecessary risk."

"You have proved that I do not know you, Lauren. Inarguably. So indulge me." If his intention was to eviscerate her, he was succeeding. Lauren wanted to curl up and whimper.

"How long is this trip going to be for?"

She'd waited too long to answer because his voice cracked like thunder across the room again.

"Who let you through here without breathing so much as a word to even Arif? I don't know what shocked me more last time, that you had managed to flee or your cunning knack in making such a convenient alliance."

Lauren flinched, remembering Rashid's words. "I'm sorry for running away like that. For taking her help. For…"

"Who helped you return?"

"If you didn't know that I was here, what were you doing in this suite then?"

In that infinitesimal moment in which he hesitated, in the dark shadows under his eyes, in his reading glasses and papers and that fountain pen of his that sat on the coffee table, Lauren found her answer.

He sat here in the dark, in the suite she had stayed in, night after night.

God, she'd been such a fool, a thousand times she could call herself that and still, it wouldn't be enough.

"Answer my question, Lauren."

"Your father. He came to New York. Brought divorce papers with him. Told me he had to get me out of your life. That he wouldn't let me ruin your great destiny."

Shock flared in his eyes.

She covered the distance between them. Willed him to look at her, to give her one chance. "He was right, about me at least. I've been selfish, foolish, but I won't let you finish this because he—"

His hands clasped her wrists and he tugged her to look up at him. And that rough, not-so-together movement of his gave Lauren courage. "*My father*… Lauren, what the hell are you talking about? I forbade him from even mentioning your name to me. I told him that he wasn't to go near you.

"And yet he…" His golden gaze flared and then went flat again. "You're here because he threatened you about the baby…" Utter defeat and a helplessness she would have never associated with him filled his face. "You believed him," his voice was raw, shaky, "that I would take our child away from you. After everything we've been through."

It was the worst she could have believed about him, and yet she had.

And that's when Lauren realized how well Rashid had played his game. How well he had manipulated Lauren, tested her and then pushed her to the truth. How well he hid so much beneath the mask of an arrogant, insufferable old man.

How easily he had done it all for Zafir…

When Zafir turned away from her, Lauren waylaid him, her heart in her throat. "His threats were empty, his words designed to flay me, showed me what I truly was. I thought he was the most insufferable man I'd ever met.

"But I didn't believe the things he said about you, Zafir. In the end, it was that simple. Because I knew you."

Zafir turned away from Lauren, a crack inching its way through his already battered heart.

His father had flown all the way to New York? Why? He knew, Zafir had warned him, that he had to stay out of his personal affairs. That he wouldn't be manipulated for Behraat or any other reason.

That his child would not become some pawn of contention between Lauren and him…

Yet he had gone and now Lauren was here, because she…

Bracing himself, he allowed himself to look at her. To let himself believe that she stood there, and was not a figment of his nightly imagination, as it had been the past month. To breathe the air she filled with that wild, lavender scent of hers.

But he would not hope again.

He would not let her cripple him further. He would not become a fool like his father and risk everything. He would not give in to the savage urge to tie her up in this very room and ensure she never left him again.

That way, lay only madness.

But *Ya Allah*, she tempted him. She'd always tempted him into madness, into selfishness, into hoping for impossible things, into gut-wrenching love that threatened to make him lose his sense of himself.

Into almost letting it all go to hell—everything his father and he had built for Behraat.

Almost.

If he did, he would never forgive himself and he would come to resent her and it would be the utter ruin he'd always wished to avoid.

Not reaching for her now was like trying to avoid the harsh, beautiful, glittering sun while standing in the middle of the desert, however.

He clamped her chin with his fingers, a primal roar threatening to burst out of him. How many times would she test him, torment him? How much lower would she bring him?

"If you believed his threats to be empty, why are you here?"

"I didn't know then. But now…" She shook her head and when she looked up, a sheen coated her midnight-black eyes. Her mouth trembled. "I…came back for you, for us. I came back because I realized what a coward I've been, Zafir. I came back because I love you so much."

Zafir stiffened, even as her words chipped away at him. He released her and fisted his hands. "You have said that before, *habeebti*. And I believed you."

He pushed his hand through his hair, feeling as weak as a leaf. And she was the gust of wind that could forever blow him away.

Her shoulders rigid, her stubborn chin lifted, she nodded. Tears fell onto her cheeks and it was all Zafir could do to not take her in his arms. But he'd reached for everything she'd offered once, believed that he could have this light, this happiness that she brought him along with Behraat.

That he needn't be alone after all for the rest of his life, with nothing but the desert and Behraat stretched before him, that he was loved.

"I know how much I hurt you." She took a bracing breath, and wiped away her tears. And he could see her heart in those brilliant eyes of hers, her courage, her honesty and her love for him. He felt ragged then, at the battle within. And for once, he desperately wanted to lose.

"I'm so new to this whole thing," she was saying then, and each step she took toward him sent his pulse racing, crumbled his will, word by word. "It was myself I didn't believe in, Zafir, not you. But now I know myself. I believe in myself and that makes what you feel for me so much clearer. Makes this wildfire between us so gut-wrenchingly simple.

"I followed you before I even understood myself, Zafir. Now…now that I can trust myself, I would follow you to the end of the world."

She pressed her mouth to his, tentative and hot and a punch to his senses. Like a kick to his gut. Like pleasure so intense and shocking that it bordered on pain.

He fell apart then. Again and again as she anchored herself on his shoulders and took his mouth with such primitive, possessive passion. Claimed him. Marked him. Undid him all over again.

But this time, he welcomed the naked, raw, powerlessness that shuddered through him. Let it wash over him, knowing that it would be all right. Gave himself over to her soft nips and strokes.

"I love you, Zafir, so much. Mere words could not encompass it all. Tell me I haven't lost my chance with you. Please tell me—" she broke then, a catch in her throat, a tremble in those deceptively slender shoulders. And Zafir took over.

In the next breath, he was devouring her, tasting her. It was his will that took over then, his love for this courageous woman that kept feeding the fire.

He picked her up and brought her to the bed. Pushed all that wild, dark hair away from her face and tilted her chin up. Tasted her roughly, deeply, desperately. "You're my heart, Lauren. You bring such joy, such light to my life, *habeebti*." He traced the lush lower lip. "Trusting in this thing between us, allowing myself to love you, it's the most terrifying thing I have done.

"But I submit to it, I choose this, I choose you like I've chosen nothing else, Lauren. I willingly become weak for you."

Nodding, she threw her arms around him. And then she cried while he held her trembling body. Like he'd never seen her.

He knew it was fear leaving her body, that she needed it and he told her that there would be nothing but light after this, that he would never ever permit her to cry like this ever again. Because he couldn't take it.

She laughed then, and looked up at him. "Ever the powerful sheikh, Zafir?" But there was only tenderness in her gaze. She took his hands in hers and brought them to her face. Kissed the center of his palm, love shining in her eyes.

"I love you, Lauren."

"I love you, too." Then she directed his hands to her belly. And his heart felt as if it would rip out of his chest. "I know, Zafir."

His breath stilled. "We agreed that we would wait."

"We argued about it and you commanded me as if that was enough," she threw back. "I know you didn't want to know, so I won't force you—"

Her name was an entreaty on his lips as he begged her

to tell him. And the minx teased him. "You're going to be the death of me, *habeebti*."

She rubbed her finger over his lips, as if she couldn't bear to not touch him. "Only if you promise that you won't tell your father. This is the only way I can pay him back."

His smile slipping from his face, Zafir tried his hardest to not scowl. "I have no idea what you're talking about. But be assured, Lauren. He's not going to have a single say in our life, in our child's life."

So Zafir hadn't forgiven Rashid and yet, he had come for her.

"It's a boy, Zafir," she breathed against his mouth. Then she wrapped her arms around his middle and kissed his chest, held him through the tremor that shook him. "A son who'll be just as handsome as his father, I hope."

He kissed her temple reverently, his mouth curved into such a beautiful smile. "I love you, Lauren," he whispered again and again, against her mouth. "You're my heart, my friend, my family, everything."

"Zafir?"

"Yes?"

"Will you do something for me?"

"Anything, Lauren. I'm yours to command."

"Try to forgive your father. Please." When he began to retreat from her, she held his hands. "He...came for you, Zafir. He...pushed me and eviscerated me...just to see if I was worthy of you. He...he knew you'd do your duty by Behraat and still, he came...only for your happiness."

"He will only make our life hard, *habeebti*. Why do you ask this for him?"

Lauren traced that aquiline nose, his brow, his sensuous mouth with trembling fingers. "For you, Zafir. Forgive him for you. Forgive him for grabbing his happiness the only way he could with your mother.

"You know, amidst all this, I realized something. It was

her choice, wasn't it? To live with him, to love him, to make a life with him the only way she could. And as to why he didn't—"

"He told me why. He was afraid for my life. So he had it put out that I died along with her and then had Arif bring me back to him when I was four."

Lauren waited, the haunted expression in his eyes twisting her. "I wish I could bear this pain for you, Zafir. I... All I can do is tell you that I love you."

His forehead leaning against hers, he smiled. "That is not a small thing you give me, Lauren. Your love is everything to me, *habeebti*. With you by my side, I can take on the entire world. Even my father."

"You. Me. Forever," she said lightly and her reward was the look of utter joy in his gaze.

EPILOGUE

KAREEM ALEXANDER AL MASOOD was born four months later, a chubby, black-haired, golden-eyed bundle that gave his father, the magnificent High Sheikh Zafir Al Masood, the fright of his life when he'd balled up his cheeks for a full five seconds and bellowed at the top of his lungs when he'd held him.

The look in Zafir's eyes every time he held Kareem and that deep, visceral smile for Lauren, it filled her with joy and gratitude.

Over that first month, true to his promise, Zafir tried his level best to spend time with their son and Lauren. Most often than not, his visit got interrupted even with all the contingencies in place.

And Lauren told herself to have patience.

Six weeks after Kareem was born, Lauren had taken a bath, dismissed the maid who was watching Kareem and settled down to feed him. It was around four and suddenly the night stretched in front of her felt long and interminable.

And then there stood Zafir looking down at her, a content smile on his face.

Lauren pressed a kiss on his hand when he cupped her face and leaned against him as he silently settled on the armrest. "Hmm… I've forgotten how good you smell," she said, trying to swallow the rush of love gathered in her throat.

She'd barely seen him this past week. Even exhausted

as she was mostly with Kareem and sleep-deprived, she had missed him so much.

They sat in silence. When Lauren finished with Kareem, Zafir took him, cuddled his son for a little longer and then called back the maid and handed him over to her, before dismissing her once again.

"Your evening is mine," he declared, pulling her out of the recliner. When she looked at the retreating maid in question, he clasped her face, his golden gaze smiling. "He'll be close, Lauren. There is a number of staff that'll be watching him. They'll bring him to us when he needs you."

Surprised, Lauren smiled and tucked herself closer into Zafir's arms. Every day, their bond only deepened. And with a million matters that he managed, Zafir still somehow understood when she needed him.

He kissed her brow, her nose, her cheek and then finally found her mouth. She groaned and pushed herself into his touch, the fire always just there simmering, waiting to be stoked. Waiting to engulf them both.

"I've missed you so much," the words escaped her and then she hid her face in his neck.

He cradled her head with one hand, while the other settled on her hip, and nudged her closer to him. Languorous fire licked through Lauren's nerves. "No, *habeebti*. Never feel ashamed for missing me, or for needing me. Never stop loving me. I miss you every day, too, Lauren."

She flattened her palms on his chest, loving the thud of his heart under it. "So, Your Highness, what do you think we should do with three whole hours?"

He flicked his tongue over her ear, his hands sinking into her shoulders. "The whole night is ours, *habeebti*. And I'm yours."

Then his hungry gaze held hers. "I was wondering if you were ready to resume your wifely duties."

When Lauren remained silent, he tilted his head. "What is it, Lauren?"

Shuddering, Lauren ran her hands over him. The washboard abdomen, the narrow hips, the rock-hard thighs... every inch of him that she missed, that she hadn't touched in so many weeks. "No, I've missed you and... I'm more than ready. It's just that..."

"Whatever it is, you can tell me, Lauren."

"I... I look different, Zafir." He didn't let her shy her gaze away and Lauren flushed even more. "My body's different. I guess—"

Without letting her finish, Zafir picked her up and carried her to the bed. "You've given me such a beautiful and apparently ferocious son," he added laughing. "You even somehow forged a bond between me and my father. You've created the family that I'd always longed for, Lauren. Have you any idea how precious you are to me?"

With the flick of his hand, he pulled something out of his pocket and held it out for her.

The antique silver glinted in the muted light, a soft tinkle from the charm hanging against it.

It was the bracelet she had haggled over in the bazaar. "How did you know?" Tears filled her eyes. "How did you find it?"

"Ahmed told me how much you had loved it. That vendor traveled on with a tribe and it took me some time to have him tracked."

He put the bracelet on her hand, and slowly unbuttoned her blouse. Lauren heard the hiss of his breath as he cupped her breasts.

One look at the dark desire in his eyes and Lauren's doubts melted away. Desperate for him, she brought her hand down to his crotch.

He was hard, ready for her. As she was for him.

The same heat flickering wild between them, Lauren let Zafir take her to dizzying heights again.

And that particular, moonlit night, their forever continued in that room with fireworks and middle-of-the-night feedings and laughter and cuddles.

* * * * *

MILLS & BOON®

MODERN™

POWER, PASSION AND IRRESISTIBLE TEMPTATION

0216/01

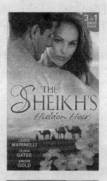

MILLS & BOON®
The Billionaires Collection!

This fabulous 6 book collection features stories from some of our talented writers. Feel the temperature rise with our ultra-sexy and powerful billionaires. Don't miss this great offer – buy the collection today to get two books free!

2 FREE BOOKS!

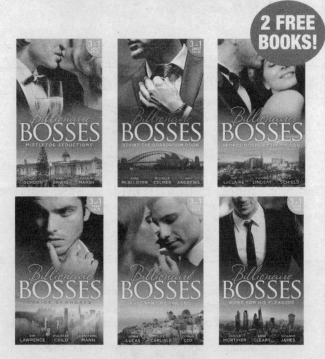

Order yours at
**www.millsandboon.co.uk
/billionaires**

MILLS & BOON®

Let us take you back in time with our Medieval Brides...

The Novice Bride – Carol Townend

The Dumont Bride – Terri Brisbin

The Lord's Forced Bride – Anne Herries

The Warrior's Princess Bride – Meriel Fuller

The Overlord's Bride – Margaret Moore

Templar Knight, Forbidden Bride – Lynna Banning

Order yours at
www.millsandboon.co.uk/medievalbrides

MILLS & BOON®

Why shop at millsandboon.co.uk?

Each year, thousands of romance readers find their perfect read at millsandboon.co.uk. That's because we're passionate about bringing you the very best romantic fiction. Here are some of the advantages of shopping at www.millsandboon.co.uk:

* **Get new books first**—you'll be able to buy your favourite books one month before they hit the shops

* **Get exclusive discounts**—you'll also be able to buy our specially created monthly collections, with up to 50% off the RRP

* **Find your favourite authors**—latest news, interviews and new releases for all your favourite authors and series on our website, plus ideas for what to try next

* **Join in**—once you've bought your favourite books, don't forget to register with us to rate, review and join in the discussions

Visit **www.millsandboon.co.uk**
for all this and more today!